On Writing

BY CHARLES BUKOWSKI,
Available from Ecco

The Days Run Away Like Wild Horses Over the Hills (1969)
Post Office (1971)
Mockingbird Wish Me Luck (1972)
South of No North (1973)
Burning in Water, Drowning in Flame: Selected Poems 1955–1973 (1974)
Factotum (1975)
Love Is a Dog from Hell (1977)
Women (1978)
You Kissed Lilly (1978)
*Play the Piano Drunk Like a Percussion Instrument until the Fingers Begin
    to Bleed a Bit (1979)*
Shakespeare Never Did This (1979)
Dangling in the Tournefortia (1981)
Ham on Rye (1982)
Bring Me Your Love (1983)
Hot Water Music (1983)
There's No Business (1984)
War All the Time: Poems 1981–1984 (1984)
You Get So Alone at Times That It Just Makes Sense (1986)
The Movie: "Barfly" (1987)
The Roominghouse Madrigals: Early Selected Poems 1946–1966 (1988)
Hollywood (1989)
Septuagenarian Stew: Stories & Poems (1990)
The Last Night of the Earth Poems (1992)
Screams from the Balcony: Selected Letters 1960–1970 (1993)
Pulp (1994)

Living on Luck: Selected Letters 1960s–1970s (Volume 2) (1995)

Betting on the Muse: Poems & Stories (1996)

Bone Palace Ballet: New Poems (1997)

The Captain Is Out to Lunch and the Sailors Have Taken Over the Ship (1998)

Reach for the Sun: Selected Letters 1978–1994 (Volume 3) (1999)

What Matters Most Is How Well You Walk Through the Fire: New Poems (1999)

Open All Night: New Poems (2000)

Night Torn Mad with Footsteps: New Poems (2001)

*Beerspit Night and Cursing: The Correspondence of Charles Bukowski &
    Sheri Martinelli 1960–1967 (2001)*

Sifting Through the Madness for the Word, the Line, the Way: New Poems (2003)

The Flash of Lightning Behind the Mountain: New Poems (2004)

Slouching Toward Nirvana (2005)

Come On In! (2006)

The People Look Like Flowers at Last (2007)

The Pleasures of the Damned (2007)

The Continual Condition (2009)

On Writing (2015)

BUK

On Writing

CHARLES BUKOWSKI

Edited by Abel Debritto

ecco

An Imprint of HarperCollinsPublishers

FIRST EDITION

Designed by Suet Yee Chong

Library of Congress Cataloging-in-Publication Data has been applied for.

ISBN 978-0-06-239600-6

15 16 17 18 19   OV/RRD   10 9 8 7 6 5 4 3 2 1

Editor's Note

It's virtually impossible to faithfully reproduce Bukowski's letters as a large number of them were profusely decorated with drawings and doodles. Similarly, all the 1945–1954 correspondence was handwritten—coincidentally enough, it was Bukowski's infamous ten-year drunk, when he misleadingly said he didn't write at all, as if all the handwritten material was forgettable—and it cannot be properly reproduced here. However, some distinctive letters have been reprinted in facsimile so that they can be appreciated as intended by Bukowski.

To further preserve Bukowski's peculiar letter writing, editorial changes have been kept to a minimum. While Bukowski's punctuation was quite accurate, his spelling was whimsical at best, and he admitted as much. In this collection, unintended typos have been silently corrected, while deliberate typos have been kept in an attempt to preserve his voice as much as possible. Likewise, salutations and closings, which were largely similar, have been omitted. Bukowski was a prolific correspondent, and his letters were usually long, discussing topics unrelated to the art of writing. Editorial omissions are then represented by [. . .]. Editorial notes in the text also appear in brackets. Bukowski used ALL CAPITALS for emphasis, and they have been replaced by italics for book titles and by quotation marks for poem and short-story titles. Dates and titles have been standardized, too. Other than these few editorial changes, these letters appear here as Bukowski wrote them.

1945

Hallie Burnett coedited Story *magazine, where Bukowski was first published in 1944.*

[To Hallie Burnett]
Late October 1945

I received your rejection of "Whitman: His Poetry and Prose," along with the informal comments of your manuscript readers.

Sounds like a nice thing.

Should you ever need an extra manuscript reader, please let me know. I can't find a job anywhere, so I might as well try you too.

1946

[To Caresse Crosby]
October 9, 1946

PHILA, PA
OCT. 9, 1946

DEAR MRS. CROSBY:

I WAS WORKING IN
A PICTURE FRAME
FACTORY

AND DRINKING,
WHEN YOU ACCEPTED
ONE OF MY STORIES

IN THE LETTER
YOU SAID, IT
"WAS PUZZLING
AND PROFOUND.

I LOST MY JOB,

MY FATHER BOUGHT
ME A NEW SUIT
AND SHIPPED ME
TO PHILADELPHIA

I LIVED ON SOCIAL
SECURITY, HAD TOO
MUCH TIME TO THINK
AND DRINK —

2

I KEPT WONDERING ABOUT PORTFOLIO.

I WROTE DIVERS CONTUMELIOUS NOTES, LOOKING UP FRENCH WORDS IN THE BACK OF MY DICTIONAIRY. I WANTED A COPY OF PORTFOLIO, WITH MY STORY IN IT. I HAD THE CRAZY BLUES, THE SUCIDIAL MANIA, THE WINE DREAMS. I NEEDED A SPIRITUAL LIFT. I WAS ENTHUSASTIC IN MY DEMANDS. AFTER SEVERAL INTERCHANGES, I GOT IT (PORTFOLIO)

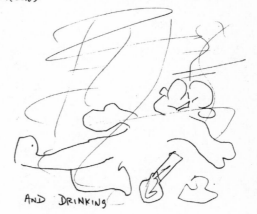

I AM NOW WORKING IN A TOOL WAREHOUSE —

AND DRINKING

3

Yet I keep wondering. Where are those stories and sketches I sent her in March 1946? Is she angry? Is this her revenge? Did she burn my things? Did she make the pages into paper boats for the bathtub? Or does Henry Miller sleep with them under his matress?

I can wait no longer.

If I receive no answer, I'll have my answer,

Truly,
Charles Bukowski
603 N. 17th. St.
Phila, 30, Pa.

[To Caresse Crosby]
November 1946

I *must* write you once more to tell you how delighted I was to receive that delicious photo—Rome 1946—and your note. As to

4

the lost manuscripts—damn them—they were no good anyhow—except maybe some violent sketches I made while sponging on my parents in Los Angeles. But such stuff to the birds: I am a poet, et al.

Drink still has me wavering—typewriter gone. Still, ha ha, I hand-print out my stuff in ink. Have managed to get rid of three fair stories and four unsatisfactory poems to *Matrix*, a rather old-fashioned Philadelphia "little magazine."

I am really a much too nervous person to hitch hike to Washington to see you. I would break up into all sorts of quatern little pieces. Thanks, really, though. You've been very decent, very.

Might send you something soon, but not for awhile. Whatever that means.

1947

[To Whit Burnett]
April 27, 1947

Thank you for the note.

I don't think I could do a novel—I haven't the urge, though I have thought about it, and someday I might try it. *Blessed Factotum* would be the title and it would be about the low-class workingman, about factories and cities and courage and ugliness and drunkenness. I don't think if I wrote it now it would be any good, though. I would have to get properly worked up. Besides, I have so many personal worries right now that I'm in no shape to look into a mirror, let alone run off a book. I am, however, surprised and pleased with your interest.

I haven't any other pen sketches, without stories, right now. *Matrix* took the only one I did that way.

The world has had little Charles pretty much by the balls of late, and there isn't much writer left, Whit. So hearing from you was damned lovely.

1953

[To Caresse Crosby]
August 7, 1953

Hello Mrs. Crosby:

Saw in book review (never really read one, but) your name, "Dail Press."

You printed me sometime back in "Portfolio," one of the earliest (1946 or so?). Well, one time came into town off long drunk, forced to live with parents during feeble clime. Thing is, parents read story ("20 TANKS FROM KASSEDOWN") and burnt whole damn "Portfolio." Now, no longer have copy. Only piece missing from my few published works. If

7

you have an extra copy ????? (and I don't see why in the hell you ~~should~~ ~~have~~ have) it would do me a lot of good if you would ship it to me.

I don't write so much now, I'm getting on to 33, pot-belly and creeping dementia. Sold my typewriter to go on a drunk 6 or 7 years ago and haven't gotten enough non-alcoholic $ to buy another. Now print my occasionals out by hand and paint them up with drawings (like any other madman). Sometimes I just throw the stories away and hang the drawings up in the bathroom (sometimes on the roller).

Hope you have "20 TANKS". Would apprec.

Love,

Charles Bukowski
268 4/6 S. Coronado St.
Los Angeles, Calif.

(268 1/6 S. CORONADO ST.)

8

Saw in book review (never really read one, but) your name, "Dail Press."

You printed me sometime back in *Portfolio,* one of the earliest (1946 or so?). Well, one time came into town off long drunk, forced to live with parents during feeble clime. Thing is, parents read story ("20 Tanks from Kasseldown") and burnt whole damn *Portfolio.* Now, no longer have copy. Only piece missing from my few published works. If you have an extra copy????? (and I don't see why in the hell you *should* have) it would do me a lot of good if you would ship it to me.

I don't write so much now, I'm getting on to 33, pot-belly and creeping dementia. Sold my typewriter to go on a drunk 6 or 7 years ago and haven't gotten enough non-alcoholic $ to buy another. Now print my occasionals out by hand and point them up with drawings (like any other madman). Sometimes I just throw the stories away and hang the drawings up in the bathroom (sometimes on the roller).

Hope you have "20 Tanks." Would appreci.

————————

[To Judson Crews]
Late 1953

You send out the only cheerful rejections in America. It's nice to have the news behind those delicious photos! You are a pretty good guy, I'd rather imagine.

I was impressed with your last edition of *Naked Ear.* It smacked of aliveness and artistry much more than, say, the latest edition of *The Kenyon Review.* That comes of printing what you *want* to print instead of printing what is *correct.* Keep it up.

Met Janet Knauff yesterday. She has met you. Took her to the races.

[To Judson Crews]
November 4, 1953

I'll be honest with you. You might as well keep those poems as long as you want to because when you do send them back I'll just throw them away.

Except for the new ones on top, these poems have been rejected by *Poetry* magazine and a new outfit, *Embryo*. Favorable remarks, etc., but they do not think my stuff is poetry. I know what they mean. The idea is there but I can't break thro the skin. I can't work the dials. I'm not interested in poetry. I don't know what interests me. Non-dullness, I suppose. Proper poetry is dead poetry even if it looks good.

Keep these things as long as you like. You're the only one who has shown an interest. If I do any more, I'll send them out to you.

1954

[To Whit Burnett]
June 10, 1954

6 – 10 – 54

Dear Mr. Burnett:

Please note change of address (323½ N. Westmoreland Ave L.A. 4.), if you are holding any more of my weird masterpieces.

rejected by Esquire

This piece is an expanded version of a short sketch I sent you some time ago. I guess it's too sexy for publication. I don't know exactly what it means. I just got to playing around with it and it ran away with me. I think Sherwood Anderson would enjoy it but he can't read it.
— Mr. Bukowski

11

Please note change of address (323½ N. Westmoreland Ave., L.A. 4), if you are holding up more of my wino masterpieces.

This piece rejected by *Esquire* is an expanded version of a short sketch I sent you some time ago. I guess it's too sexy for publication. I don't know exactly what it means. I just got to playing around with it and it ran away with me. I think Sherwood Anderson would enjoy it but he can't read it.

[To Whit Burnett]
August 25, 1954

I'm sorry to hear, through a slip sent me from Smithtown a couple of months back, that *Story* is no longer alive.

I sent in another story about that time called "The Rapist's Story," but haven't heard. Is it about?

I'll always remember the old orange magazine with the white band. Somehow, I'd always had the idea that I could write anything I wanted, and, if it was good enough it'd get in there. I've never gotten that idea looking at any other magazines, and especially today, when everybody's so god damned afraid of offending or saying anything against anybody else—an honest writer is in a hell of a hole. I mean, you sit down to write it and you know it's no use. There's a lot of courage gone now and a lot of guts and a lot of clearness—and a lot of Artistry too.

For my money, everything went to hell with World War 2. And not only the Arts. Even cigarettes don't taste the same. Tamales. Chili. Coffee. Everything's made of plastic. A radish doesn't taste sharp anymore. You peel an egg and, invariably, the egg comes off with the shell. Pork chops are all fat and pink. People buy new cars and nothing else. That's their life: four wheels. Cities only turn on one-third of their street lights to save electricity. Policemen give out tickets like mad. Drunks are fined atrocious sums, and almost everybody's drunk who's had a drink. Dogs must be kept on a leash, dogs must be inoculated. You have to have a fishing license to catch grunion with your hands, and comic books are considered dangerous to children. Men watch boxing matches from their armchairs, men who never knew what a boxing match was, and when they disagree with a decision, they write vile and clamorous letters to the newspapers in protest indignant.

And short stories: there's nothing: no life. [. . .]

Story had meant something to me. And I guess it's part of the world's ways to see it go, and I wonder what's going to be next?

I remember when I used to write and send you fifteen or twenty or more stories a month, and later, three or four or five—and mostly, at *least,* one a week. From New Orleans and Frisco and Miami and L.A. and Philly and St. Louis and Atlanta and Greenwich Village and Houston and everyplace else.

I used to sit up by an open window in New Orleans and look down at the summer streets of night and touch those keys, and when I sold my typewriter in Frisco to get drunk on, I couldn't stop writing, and I couldn't stop drinking either, so I hand-printed my crap out in ink for years, and later decorated same crap with drawings to make you notice them.

Well, they tell me I can't drink now, and I've got another typewriter. I've got a job of a sort now but don't know how long I'll hold it. I'm weak and I get sick easy, and I'm nervous all the time and guess I've got a couple of short-circuits somewhere, but with it, I feel like touching those keys again, touching them and making lines, a stage, a set-up, making people walk and talk and close doors. And now, there's no more *Story.*

But I want to thank you, Burnett, for bearing with me. I know a lot of it was poor. But those were good days, the days of 438

Fourth Ave. 16, and now like everything else, the cigarettes and the wine and the cock-eyed sparrows in the half-moon, it's all gone. A sorrow heavier than tar. Goodbye, goodbye.

[To Caresse Crosby]
December 9, 1954

I received your letter from Italy a year or so ago (in response to mine). I wish to thank you for remembering me. It built me up some to hear from you.

Are you still publishing? If so, I have something I'd like you to see. And if you are, I'd like an address to send it to: I don't know how to reach you.

I'm writing again, a little. [Charles] Shattuck of *Accent* says he doesn't see how I can find a publisher for my stuff, but that perhaps someday "public taste will catch up with you." Christ.

You sent me a pamphlet of a sheaf or something in Italian last year in your letter. You have mistaken me for an educated man: I couldn't read it. I am not even a real artist—know I am a fake of some sort—sort of write from the bowels of disgust, almost entirely. Yet, when I see what the others are doing, I go on with it. What else is there to do? [. . .]

This factotum has another menial job. I hate it, but I have two pairs of shoes for the first time in my life (I like to doll up for the track—playact for the real railbird character). I have been living for the past 5 years with a woman 10 years older than I. But I have gotten used to her and I am too tired to search or to break.

Please let me have your editorial address if you are still publishing, and thank you again for being kind enough to remember me and write.

1955

[To Whit Burnett]
February 27, 1955

Thank you for the return of old stories; and the enclosed note.

I'm doing a little better now, though I almost died in the charity ward of the General Hospital. They sure mess up there, and if you've ever heard anything about the place, it's probably true. I was there 9 days and they sent me a bill for $14.24 a day. Some charity ward. Wrote a story about it called "Beer, Wine, Vodka, Whiskey; Wine, Wine, Wine" and sent it to *Accent*. They sent it back: . . . "quite a bloody spate. Perhaps, some day, public taste will catch up with you."

My God. I hope not. [. . .]

By the way, in your note you said you had never printed me. Do you have a copy of *Story*, March-April 1944?

Well, I'm 34 now. If I don't make it by the time I'm 60, I'm just going to give myself 10 more years.

1956

The poem "A Note to Carl Sandburg" remains unpublished; A Place to Sleep the Night *was abandoned after Doubleday rejected a few chapters.*

[To Carol Ely Harper]
November 13, 1956

The poems you mentioned are still available—I do not keep carbons and so do not recall the poems completely but am particularly pleased with your accepting "A Note to Carl Sandburg." This is a poem I wrote mostly to myself, not thinking anybody would have the courage to publish it.

I am 36 years old (8-16-20) and was first published (a short story) in Whit Burnett's *Story* mag back in 1944. Then a few stories and poems in 3 or 4 issues of *Matrix* about the same time, and a story in *Portfolio*. As you know, these mags are now deceased. And, oh yes, a story and a couple of poems in something called *Write* that came out once or twice and then gave it up. Then for 7 or 8 years I wrote very, very little. It was quite a drunk. I ended up in the charity ward of the hospital with holes in my belly, heaving up blood like a waterfall. I took a 7 pint continuous transfusion—and lived. I am not the man I used to be but I'm writing again.

Received a note from Spain yesterday from Mrs. Hills informing me that one of my poems has been accepted for *Quixote*. And I am to have some stories and poems featured in the next edition of *Harlequin,* a new magazine that put out its first copy in Texas and has now moved to L.A. They have asked me to join the editorial staff which I have done. And it is quite an experience; and this is what I have learned: that there are so many, *many* writers writing that can't write at all, and they keep right on writing all the clichés and bromides, and 1890 plots, and poems about Spring and poems about Love, and poems they think are modern because they are done in slang or staccato style, or written with all the "i's" small, or, or, *or!!!* . . . Well, you see, I can't join the *Experiment Group* but I am honored that you might have asked me in. There simply—as you must know from your nervous breakdown—isn't enough time—I have my trivial, tiring, low-paying job 44 hours a week, and I am going to night school 4 nights a week, two hours a night, plus an added hour or two home work. I am taking a course in Commercial Art for the next couple of years, if I last (this is the night school deal), and besides this, I have just started my first novel, *A Place to Sleep the Night.* I am being very profuse in telling you all this, so if I *don't* send you a couple of one-minute plays, you'll know why. However, if I know myself, you will get some attempts from me. I don't think, though, that the play-form stirs me as it should. We'll see.

1958

The four poems mentioned below were printed in the first issue of Nomad *in 1959.*

[To the editors of *Nomad*]
September 1958

I am gratified that you found 4 poems that you liked. This is quite a wholesale number and a shot in the arm for quite some time to come. Either the poetry field is opening up or I am, or we both are. Anyhow, it's nice, and I must allow myself a feeling of niceness once in a while. [. . .]

About me, I must seem pretty old to be about beginning in poetry: I was 38 on this last August 16th and feel, look and act a hell of a lot older. I've been working with poetry the last couple of years after about a 10 year blank, self-inflicted I suppose, and rather unhappy but not without its moments. I'm not one to look back on wanton waste as complete loss—there's music in everything, even defeat—but coming up on a death bed in a charity ward slowed me somewhat, gave me the old pause to think. I found myself writing poetry: hell of a state. I had been, in my earlier days, working with the short story, getting quite a bit of encouragement from Whit Burnett discoverer of W[illiam] Saroyan and others and founder of the then famous *Story* magazine. Whit finally took one—I used to send him 15 or 20 stories a month and when they came back, I would tear them up—back in 1944 when I was sweet, fiery and 24. I landed 3 or 4 stories in *Matrix* and one in an international review of the time called *Portfolio,* and then I more or less tossed everything overboard, until a couple of years back when I began writing poetry exclusively. For the first year nobody bit and then I was published (and this brings us up to date) in *Quixote, Harlequin, Existaria, The Naked Ear, The Beloit Poetry Journal, Hearse, Approach, The Compass Review* and *Quicksilver.* I have work accepted for future publication in *Insert, Quixote, Semina, Olivant, Experiment, Hearse, Views, The Coercion Review, Coastlines, Gallows* and *The San Francisco Review. Hearse* is bringing out a chapbook of my poems *Flower, Fist and Bestial Wail* early next year . . . I went to L.A. City College when I was a kid and took a course in journalism but the nearest I've gotten to a newspaper is every 2 or 3 days when I flip through one without too damned much interest. Went back to night school there about a year ago and took some art courses, commercial and otherwise but then too, they moved too slow for me and wanted too much obeisance. I have no definite talent or trade, and how I stay alive is largely a matter of magic. That's about it—you can take the few lines you need out of here.

1959

[To Anthony Linick]
March 6, 1959

[. . .] I should think that many of our poets, the honest ones, will confess to having no manifesto. It is a painful confession but the art of poetry carries its own powers without having to break them down into critical listings. I do not mean that poetry should be raffish and irresponsible clown tossing off words into the void. But the very feeling of a good poem carries its own reason for being. I am aware of the New Criticism and the Newer Criticism and the Blue Guitar school of thought, the English school forwarded by Paris Leary, the strong image school of *Epos* and *Flame,* etc. etc., but all these are demands on style and manner and method rather than on content, although we have some restrictions here also. But primarily Art is its own excuse, and it's either Art or it's something else. It's either a poem or a piece of cheese.

Bukowski's "Manifesto: A Call for Our Own Critics" appeared in Nomad *5/6 in 1960.*

[To Anthony Linick]
April 2, 1959

20

[. . .] While writing, I should mention that the "manifesto" essay I sent yesterday (I believe) is now bothering me. Although I do not have the script around, I believe I used the phrase "leave us be fair." This has been keeping me awake upon my hot lonely pad (the whores are laying with less involved fools as of now). I believe "let us be fair" is more correct. Or is it? Any grammarians on *Nomad*? In my youth (ah lo, swift the years!) I received a D in English I at dear old L.A.C.C. for showing up every morning at 7:30 a.m. with a hangover. It wasn't the hangover so much as the fact that the class began at 7:00 a.m., usually with a rendering blast from Gilbert and Sullivan, which, I am sure, would have killed me. In English II I received an A or a B because the teacher was a female who caught me constantly looking at her legs. All of which is to say, I didn't pay a hell of a lot of attention to grammar, and when I write it is for the love of the word, the color, like tossing paint on a canvas, and using a lot of ear and having read a bit here and there, I generally come out ok, but technically I don't know what's happening, nor do I care. Let us be fair. let us be fair. Let us . . .

[To Anthony Linick]
April 22, 1959

[. . .] I must rush off now to catch the first race. Thank you for lessening the blow on my weakness of grammar by mentioning that some of your college friends have trouble with sentence structure. I think some writers do suffer this fate mainly because at heart they are rebellious and the rules of grammar like many of the other rules of our world call for a herding in and a confirmation that the natural writer instinctively abhors, and, furthermore, his interest lies in the wider scope of subject and spirit . . . Hemingway, Sherwood Anderson, Gertrude Stein, Saroyan were a few that reshaped the rules, especially in punctuation and sentence flow and breakdown. And, of course, James Joyce went even further. We are interested in color, shape, meaning, *force*... the pigments that point up the soul. But I feel that there is a difference between being a non-grammarian and being unread, and it is the unread and the unprepared, those so hasty to splash into print that they have not reached into the ages for a sound and basic springboard, that I take task with. And most certainly the *Kenyon Review* school has the edge on us here, although they have gone so far overboard on this point that their creative edge is dulled.

James Boyer May edited and published Trace, *where excerpts from Bukowski's correspondence appeared in several issues.*

[To James Boyer May]
Early June 1959

[...] As to those who have some doubt as to my psychological fitness, I feel this stems from a misconception of my poetic intent. I have not worked out my poems with a careful will, falling rather on haphazard and blind formulation of wordage, a more flowing concept, in a hope for a more new and lively path. I do personalize, at times, but this only for the grace and élan of the dance.

The four Bukowski poems published in Nomad *1 were unfavorably reviewed in* Trace *32 by William J. Noble (1959).*

[To Anthony Linick]
July 15, 1959

Privately now, I would like to comment to you on the Noble Bitch in *Trace* 32. Why this eltchl, this conservative from the halls of the ikons and holy rollers, the pluckers of rondeaux and smellers of lilies, why this spalpeen should set himself up as a special critic of literary know-how is more than I can dispense with with a quodlibet. I need a stronger antiseptic.

The field boils with literary journals, a great slough and potwash of them for those who wish to continue on the descensive, whether they be gnostics, pansies or grandmothers who keep canaries and goldfish. Why these reactionaries cannot be content with their lot, why they must lacerate us with their yellow-knuckled souls, the looming kraken of their god-head, is beyond me. I certainly do not give a magniloquent damn what they print in *their* journals: I beg no alms for modern verse. Yet they came bickering to us. Why? Because they smell life and cannot stand it, they want to plunge us into the same spume and sputum that has held them daft with the deism of stale 1890 verse.

Mr. Noble believes I am being brash and sexy when I speak of "fumbling with flat breasts." There is nothing less sexy, though certainly there are things less brash. It is a tragedy of poetry and life, these flat breasts, and those of us who *live* life as well as write about it must realize that if we outstay our feelings on this we might as well ignore the fall of Rome, or ignore cancer, or the piano works of Chopin. And, "shooting craps with God" will be about the only game left when the air is regaled with purple flashes and the mountains open mouths to roar and the splendid rockets promise only a landing in hell.

Perhaps I'm being indiscriminate in not digesting Mr. Noble.

23

But his perturbation over things that do not seem like alikeness, perhaps points that the selfishness lies elsewhere. I have made the conservative journals with conservative verse but I have not bade them, "come, do my beckoning!" I've merely smiled, thought, I've landed in the camp of the enemy, laid their broads, played with breasts both flat and deliciously not-so-flat, and stolen away, unmarked, uncaged, still rapacious in nature, stag, snarling and ingenious. I suppose this is what Mr. Noble was referring to when he said "Mr. Bukowski has a talent." It was very kind of him. And I enjoyed the less-flat breasts.

[To James Boyer May]
December 13, 1959

The other night I was visited by an editor and a writer (Stanley McNail of *The Galley Sail Review* and Alvaro Cardona-Hine) and the fact that they found me in a disordered and disheveled state is by no means completely my fault: the visit was as unannounced as an H-Bomb attack. My question is this: does a writer become public property to be ransacked without notice upon publication or does he still retain the rights of privacy as a tax-paying citizen? Would it be gross to say that the only eucharist of many an artist is (still) isolation from an only too-fast closing society, or is this simply a desuetude?

I do not feel it is pedantic or ignoble to demand freedom from the opiate of clannishness and leech-brotherhood that dominates many many of our so-called avant-garde publications.

. . . Well, the editor at least had a beer with me, although the writer would have none—so I drank for the both of us. We discussed Villon, Rimbaud and Baudelaire's *Flowers of Evil*. (It seemed a very French night with both of my visitors being very careful to use the French title for B's works.) We also discussed J. B. May, Hedley, Poots, Cardona-Hine and Charles Bukowski. We impugned and maligned and encircled. Finally fatigued the editor and writer arose. I lied, said it had been nice to see them, the gillies and the morels, the gimblets and the glimpes, the lulling light of Lucifer. They left, and I cracked another beer, clouted with the rakishness of modern American editorialism. . . . If this be writing, if this be poesy, I ask a helminthagogun: I've earned $47 in 20 years of writing and I think that $2 a year (omitting stamps, paper, envelopes, ribbons, divorces and typewriters) entitles one to the special privacy of a special insanity and if I need hold hands with paper gods to promote a little scurvy rhyme, I'll take the encyst and paradise of rejection.

[To James Boyer May]
December 29, 1959

[. . .] I have often taken the isolationist stand that all that matters is the creation of the poem, the pure art form. What my character is or how many jails I have lounged in, or wards or walls or wassails, how many lonely-heart poetry readings I have dodged is beside the point. A man's soul or lack of it will be evident with what he can carve upon a white sheet of paper. And if I can see more poetry in the Santa Anita stretch or drunk under the banana tree than in a smoky room of lavender rhyming, that is up to me and only time will judge which climate was proper, not some jackass second-rate editor afraid of a printer's bill and trying to ham it on subscriptions and coddling contributions. If the boys are trying to make a million, there's always the market, the lonely widows of the John Dillinger approach.

Let's not find out some day that Dillinger's poetry was better than ours and the *Kenyon Review* was right. Right now, under the banana tree, I'm beginning to see sparrows where I once saw hawks, and their song is not too bitter to me.

1960

[To James Boyer May]
January 2, 1960

[. . .] yes, the "littles" are all an irresponsible bunch (most of them) guided by young men, eager with the college flush, actually hoping to cut a buck from the thing, starting with fiery ideals and large ideas, long explanatory rejection slips, and dwindling down, finally, to letting the manuscripts stack behind the sofa or in the closet, some of them lost forever and never answered, and finally putting out a tacked-together, hacked-together poor selection of typographically botched poems before getting married and disappearing from the scene with some comment like "lack of support." Lack of support? Who in the hell are *they* to get it? What have they done but camouflage themselves behind the façade of Art, think up the name of a magazine, get it listed and wait for submissions from the same 2 or 3 hundred tired names that seem to think they are the poets of America because some 22 year-old jackass with a bongo drum and a loose 50 dollar bill accepts their worst poetry.

———

[To Guy Owen]
Early March 1960

It is possible to be "conservative" and still publish good poetry. So much of the "modern" has a hard shell-like blatantness that can be done by young men without background or feeling (see *Hearse*). There are false poets in all schools, people who simply do not belong. But they eventually disappear because the forces of life absorb them with something else. Most poets are young simply because they have not been caught up. Show me an old poet and I'll show you, more often than not, either a madman or a master. And, I suppose, painters too. I am a little hesitant here, and though I paint, it is not my field. But I suppose it is similar, and I am thinking of an old French janitor at one of the last places I was employed. A part-time janitor, bent of back, wine-drinking. I found he painted. Painted through a mathematical formula, a philosophical computation of life. He wrote it down before he painted it. A gigantic plan, and painted to it. He spoke of conversations with Picasso. And I had to rather laugh. There we were, a shipping clerk and a janitor discussing theories in aesthetics while all about us men drawing 10 times our salaries were lost out on the limb reaching for rotten fruit. What does this say for the American way of life?

[To Jon E. Webb]
August 29, 1960

[. . .] In case you want bio . . . you can sift it down from this mess. Born 8-16-20, Andernach, Germany, can't speak a word of German, English bad too. Editors say, no reason, Bukowski, you

28

can't spell or type correctly or have to keep using the same damned ribbon. Well, they don't know that that ribbon got tangled with my navel cord and I've been trying to get back to the mother ever since. And I don't feel like spelling . . . I think words more beautiful cannon power misspelled. Anyhow, I am old man now. 40. More mixed with mortar of scream and dizzy plight than when 14 and old man whipped ass to sundry unclassical tunes. Where were we? Let me tilt this beer again . . . heard from *Targets* this morning. Took 6 poems for December issue . . . "Horse on Fire," "Pull Me Thru the Temples" and other crap. Have another poem, "Japanese Wife," for Sept. issue. This is nice and will allow me to live 3 or 4 weeks longer. I mention this because it makes me happy in my way and I am drinking beer now. It is not so much for the fame of publication but more the good feeling that you are not perhaps insane and some of the things you say are understood. This beer is so damned good looking thru the sunny window, ho, ho, no damn women around, no short-nose horses, no cancer, no Rimbaud or DeMass rotting of siff, just orange flowers without bees and the rotting calif. grass over the rotting calif. bones. Now wait. Crack another beer. I'm going down to Del Mar for 3 or 4 days and get the rent money, figured out a new code for shortnoses.

Let's start another paragraph. Ger[trude] Stein would have told me that. But what's Ger St. is something else. We are all right in our ways only some of us have the help of the bees and the gods and the moons and the tigers yawning in the tremendous dark caves filled with Serg[ei] Rachmaninoff and César Franck and photos of [Aldous] Huxley talking to [D. H.] Lawrence over spilled wine. God dam it: bio, bio, bio . . . I hate myself, but must get on. This is blahbuk, well, christ, I dunno, I slugged the old man one night when I was drunk, 17, headed out of town. He didn't fight back and it made me sick because that was part of me . . . staring up from the couch, weak coward. I traveled all over this rotten U. states working for nothing so others could have something. I am not a commy, I am nothing political but it is a bad setup. Worked in slaughterhouse, dog biscuit factory, Di Pinna's of Miami beach, copy boy on the New Orleans' *Item,* blood bank in Frisco, hung posters in New York subways 40 feet below the sky drunk hopping beautiful golden third rails, cotton in Berdo, tomatoes; shipping clerk, truck driver, horseplayer ordinary, holder down of barstools throughout a dull alarmclock nation, supported by shackjob whores; foreman for American newsco., New York, Sears-Roebuck stock boy, gas station attendant, mailman . . . I can't remember them all, it's all rather drab and common and any man you see next to you in the unemployment line has done the same things. [. . .]

Where were we??? Christ. Anyhow, during all this, I wrote a poem or 2, published in *Matrix,* and then lost interest in poetry. Started fucking with the short story. By the way, got a letter from [Evelyn] Thorne who prints a lot of my more fancy and classical poetry—ho shit, I can write any old way, I am no good—cussing me for ussing bad langwich. Now wait. Let's see. The short story. Whit Burnett of the old *Story* mag printed my first one in 1944. I was a 24 year old kid then living in Greenwich Village and realizing the first day that the Village was dead, a signpost that someone had once been there. Shit, the mockery. Got a letter from a lady agent asking me to lunch and drinks . . . wants to talk to me and agent my stuff. Told her I couldn't meet her, wasn't ready, couldn't write, and goodbye, had my own drink under bed in form of wine bottle. Ended up in a Father Divine place 6 o'clock in the morning, drunk, locked outa room, freezing in shirt sleeves. You didn't ask for a bio, did you, Webb? In fact, whata hell, you ant even accepted onea ma pomes?

Well, anyhow, short story here and there, not too many accepted. I would send airmail to *Atlantic Monthly* and if not accepted would tear up. I don't know how many thousand masterpieces I tore up. Pro none. Various people on way try to get me to do novel. Fuck 'em. I wouldn't do novel for Khrushchev. Forget everything for awhile, 10, 15 years didn't write. Couldn't pass Cichristarist to get in Army. Good feeling. Had shorts on backwards but not intentional after 4 week drunk. They thot I was nuts, the crazy sunkabitches!

Well, look here, Wegg, I mean Webb, let me drag another beer. I am wondering about you going 21 days without a drink, this has to STOP. I ended up once in charity ward of general hospital . . . hemorrhaging blood out like fountain from ass and mouth . . . they let me lie for 2 days before they touched me, then got idea I had connections with the underworld and pumped 7 pints of blood and 8 pints of glucose into me without stopping. They told me if I ever drank again I was dead. 13 days later I was driving a truck, lifting 50 pound packages and drinking cheap wine full of sulphur. They missed the point: I *wanted* to die. And as some suicides have experienced: the human frame *can* be tougher than steel.

Now what a minute Webb w where we?

Anyhow, I came off this blackout 10, 15 year drunk, shack jobs, terror, walnuts in the sheets, walnut shells, mice leaping like rockets thru rooms 3 weeks behind in rent thru hangover dreams, green potatoes, purple bread, the love of fat grey women to make you cry their large potato bellies and dry love and rosary under pillow and photos of children impure . . . nothing to make a man feel savage and daring because he simply wants to strange himself. The women were better than we. Every last one of them. There is no such thing as a whore. I have been robbed and slugged and crabbed with the rest of them, I say, there is no such thing as a whore. Women are not built that way. Men are. The term is whoredom. I was one. Still am. But let's get on.

31

Anyway, ten or 15 years later I began to write again . . . at age 35, but this time it came out all POETRY. What the hell? The way I saw it—it saved the words . . . Ger. would have liked that, altho I am wasting a lot of words here, I am sure I will be forgiven . . . because somebody has on his power mower and WHIRRRRR CLICKWHRRIRR, it is all right with all the sun coming in and there's something on the radio . . . I don't know what . . . might have heard it only once or 2twice, so tired of the same . . . Beethoven, Brahms, Bach, Tchaikovsky, etc . . .

Anyhow, I came on with the little pome because I liked it and it seemed ok. Now I am getting a little tired and don't know quite what.

Anyhow, published here and there, drawer fulla little mags where shirts should be.

I would like to say that I have or *had* some gods—Ezra P. before I started corres. with an ex-mistress [Sheri Martinelli] . . . There's still, however, [Robinson] Jeffers. Eliot seemed to me an opportunist, going where the slickest gods gave the quietest gifts, which is great and gentile, but not human and the roar of blood or some bum dying on skid row in underwear which has not been washed for 4 weeks. I am not exactly knocking Eliot, I am knocking education and its false teeth. I could and can get more knowledge of life by talking to a garbage man than I could by talking to T.S., or for that matter, to you, Jon E. W. Where were we? [. . .]

Look, Jon, I hope you can fin' a pome. Somewhere among the bloody tunes . . . I dunno, I'm tired . . . everyplace people water lawns . . . good deal. Well, look, this was the bio.

lost my pen,

let's knock 'em dead with Alcatraz ramble . . .

Stefanile published a Bukowski poem in The Sparrow *14 (1960).*

[To Felix Stefanile]
September 19, 1960

No "bookworm or sissy" am I . . .

Your criticism correct: poem submitted was loose, sloppy, repetitive, but here's the kernel: I cannot WORK at a poem. Too many poets work too consciously at their stuff and when you see their work in print, they seem to be saying . . . see here, old man, just look at this POEM. I might even say that a poem should *not be* a poem, but more a chunk of something that happens to come out right. I do not believe in technique or schools or sissies . . . I believe in grasping at the curtains like a drunken monk . . . and tearing them down, down, down . . .

I hope to submit to you again, and believe me, I far more appreciate criticism than "sorry" or "no" or "overstocked."

[To Jon Webb]
Late September 1960

[. . .] Also got your new card today, must agree with you that one can talk poetry away and your life away, and I get more out of being around people—if I have to—who never heard of Dylan or Shakey or Proust or Bach or Picasso or Remb. or color wheels, or what. I know a couple of fighters (one with 8 win streak going), a horseplayer or two, a few whores, x-whores, and the alcoholics; but poets are bad on the digestion and sensibility, and I could make it stronger, but then they are probably better than I make them, and there is a lot of wrong in me. [. . .]

Agree with you on "poetic poetry," and rather feel that almost all poetry written, past and present, is a failure because the intent, the slant and accent, is not a carving like stone or eating a good sandwich or drinking a good drink, but more like somebody saying, "Look, I have written a poem . . . see my POEM!"

———————

[To W. L. Garner]
November 9, 1960

[. . .] I believe that too much poetry is being written as "poetry" instead of concept. By this I mean we try too hard to make these things *sound* like poems. It was Nietzsche who said when asked about the poets: "The Poets? The Poets lie too much!" The poem-form, by tradition, allows us to say much in little space, but most of us have been saying *more* than we feel, or when we lack the ability to see or carve, we substitute poetic diction, of which the word STAR is nabob and chief executor.

———————

[To Jon Webb]
December 11, 1960

[. . .] You long ago told me that you were rejecting "names" right and left. It appears then that you are selecting what you like, which is only what any editor can do. I was once an editor of *Harlequin* and have an idea of what comes along in the way of poetry—how much poorly written amateur unoriginal pretensive poetry one can get in the mails. If printing "names" means printing good poetry . . . it is up to the non-names to write poetry good enough to get in. To merely reject "names" and print 2nd. hand poetry of unknowns . . . is that what they want? . . . a form of new inferiority? Should we throw away Beethoven and Van Gogh for the musical ditties or dabblings of the lady across the street because nobody knows her name? While I was with *Harlequin* we were only able to publish ONE formerly unpublished poet, a 19 year-old boy out of Brooklyn, if I remember. And this . . . only by cutting away whole sections of the 3 or 4 poems he sent in. And after that, he never again sent in anything even partially worthwhile. And we got our letters too, bitter letters of complaint from known and unknown too. I would stay up half the night writing 2 or 3 page rejections of why I felt the poems wouldn't do—this instead of writing "sorry, no.," or the out of the printed rejection. But the sleep lost was in vain; the poems I did not write, I should have written; the drunks, the plays, the racetracks I missed, I should not have missed; the operas, the symphonies . . . because all I got back for TRYING, trying to be decent and warm and open . . . were snarling bitter letters, full of cursing and vanity and war. I would not have minded a solid analysis of my wrongs— but the sniveling, snarling missives—no, hell no. It's very odd, I thought, how people can be so very "shitty" (to use one of their terms) and write poetry too. But now, after meeting a few of them, I know that it is entirely possible. And I do not mean the clean fight, the rebel, the courage; I mean thin-minded glory-grabbers, money-mad, spiritually dwarfed.

35

In "Horse on Fire," published in Targets *4 in 1960, Bukowski puts* Pound's Cantos *down.*

[To W. L. Garner and Lloyd Alpaugh]
Late December 1960

[. . .] Old Ez[ra Pound] will probably spit out his teeth when he reads "Horse on Fire," but even the great can sometimes live in error and it is up to us smaller ones to correct their table manners. And Sheri Martinelli will wail, but why did they blubber over their precious canto and then tell me about it? I am a dangerous man when turned loose with a typewriter.

1961

[To Jon Webb]
Late January 1961

[. . .] It's when you begin to lie to yourself in a poem in order to simply *make* a poem, that you fail. That is why I do not rework poems but let them go at first sitting, because if I have lied originally there's no use driving the spikes home, and if I haven't lied, well hell, there's nothing to worry about. I can read some poems and just sense how they were shaved and riveted and polished together. You get a lot of poetry like that now out of *Poetry* Chicago. When you flip the pages, nothing but butterflies, near bloodless butterflies. I am actually shocked when I go through this magazine because nothing is happening. And I guess that's what they think a poem is. Say, something not happening. A neat lined something, so subtle you can't even feel it. This makes the whole thing intelligent art. Balls! The only thing intelligent about a good art is if it shakes you alive, otherwise it's hokum, and how come it's hokum and in *Poetry* Chi? You tell me.

In 1956 when I first began writing poetry at the doddering age of 35 after spitting my stomach out through my mouth and ass, and I have sense enough not to drink any more whiskey although a lady claimed I was staggering around her place last Friday night drinking port wine—in 1956 I sent *Experiment* a handful of poems that (which) they accepted, and now 5 years later they tell me they are

37

going to publish one of them, which is delayed reaction if I ever saw any. They tell me it will be out in June 1961 and I guess when I read it, it will be like an epitaph. And then she suggested I send her ten dollars and join the *Experiment Group*. Naturally, I declined. Christ, an extra ten today on Togetherness in the middle races would have had me whistling dixie through my anus.

Corrington tells me he thinks Corso and Ferlinghetti have it. I am not really as well read as I should be. But I think the modern poet must have the stream of modern life in him, and we can no longer write like Frost or Pound or Cummings or Auden, they seem a little off track as if they have fallen out of step. For my money, Frost was always out of step and has gotten away with too much malarkey. And sure, they set him up like a dead dummy in the snow and let him blubber through his dying sight and insight at the inauguration. Very fine, indeed. And any more things like that and I'm going to try and look up a Communist party card or an old black arm band or some queer to flub me off any way he likes. I hope I never get so old that I can no longer remember, but, of course, Frost has always played the favorite, and if he ever did like a 60 to one longshot, he kept his mouth shut. [. . .]

There was the time in Atlanta when I could barely see the end of the light cord—it was cut off and there wasn't any bulb and I was in a paper shack over the bridge—one dollar and 25 cents a week rent—and it was freezing and I was trying to write but mostly I wanted something to drink and my California sunlight was a long ways away, and I thought well hell, I'll get a little warmth and I reached up and I grabbed the wires in my hand but they were dead and I walked outside and stood under a frozen tree and watched through a warm frosty glass window some grocer selling some woman a loaf of bread and they stood there for ten minutes talking about nothing, and I watched them and I said I swear I swear, to *hell* with it!, and I looked up at the frozen white tree and its branches didn't point anywhere, only into a sky that didn't know my name, and it told me then: I do not know you and you are nothing. And how I felt that. If there are gods, their business is not to torture and test us to see if we are fit for the future but to do us some god damned god good in the present. The future's only a bad hunch; Shakespeare told us that—we'd all go flying there otherwise. But it's only when a man gets to the point of a gun in his mouth that he can see the whole world inside of his head. Anything else is conjecture, conjecture and bullshit and pamphlets.

———————

[To Jon Webb]
March 25, 1961

[. . .] what bothers me is when I read about the old Paris groups, or somebody who knew somebody in the old days. They did it then too, the names of old and now. I think Hemingway's writing a book about it now. But in spite of it all, I can't buy it. I can't stand writers or editors or anybody who wants to talk Art. For 3 years I lived in a skid row hotel—before my hemorrhage—and got drunk every night with an x-con, the hotel maid, an Indian, a gal who looked like she wore a wig but didn't, and 3 or 4 drifters. Nobody knew Shostakovich from Shelley Winters and we didn't give a damn. The main thing was sending runners out for liquor when we ran dry. We'd start low on the line with our worst runner and if he failed—you must understand, most of the time there was little or no money—we'd go a little deeper with our next best man. I guess it's bragging but I was top dog. And when the last one staggered through the door, pale and shamed, Bukowski would rise with an invective, don his ragged cloak and stroll with anger and assurance into the night, down to Dick's Liquor Store, and I conned him and forced him and squeezed him until he was dizzy; I would walk in in big anger, not beggary, and ask for what I wanted. Dick never knew whether I had any money or not. Sometimes I fooled him and had money. But most of the time I didn't. But anyhow, he'd slap the bottles in front of me, bag them, and then I'd pick them up with an angry, "Put 'em on my tab!"

And then he'd start the old dance—but, jesus, u owe me such and such already, and you haven't paid anything off in a month and—

And then came the ACT OF ART. I already had the bottles in my hand. It would be nothing to walk out. But I'd slap them down again in front of him, ripping them out of the bag and shoving them toward him, saying, "Here, you *want* these things! I'll take my god damned business somewhere else!"

"No, no," he'd say, "take them. It's all right."

And then he'd get out that sad slip of paper and add onto the total.

"Lemme see that," I'd demand.

And then I'd say, "For Christ's sake! I don't owe you *this* much! What's this item here?"

All this was to make him believe that I was going to pay someday. And then he'd try to con me back: "You're a gentleman. You're not like the others. I trust you."

He finally got sick and sold his business, and when the next one came in I started a new tab . . .

And what happened? At eight o'clock one Sunday morning— EIGHT O'CLOCK!!! gd damn it—there was a knock on the door— and I opened it and there stood an editor. "Ah, I'm so and so, editor of so and so, we got your short story and thought it most unusual; we are going to use it in our Spring number." "Well, come on in," I'd had to say, "but don't stumble over the bottles." And then I sat there while he told me about his wife who thought a lot of him and about his short story that had once been published in *The Atlantic Monthly,* and you know how they talk on. He finally left, and a month or so later the hall phone rang and somebody wanted Bukowski, and this time it was a woman's voice, "Mr. Bukowski, we think you have a very unusual short story and the group was discussing it the other night, but we think it has one weakness and we thought you might want to correct the weakness. It was this: WHY DID THE CEN-TRAL CHARACTER BEGIN TO DRINK IN THE FIRST PLACE?"

I said, "Forget the whole thing and send the story back," and I hung up.

When I walked back in the Indian looked up over his drink and asked "Who was it?"

I said, "Nobody," which was the most accurate answer I could give.

[To John William Corrington]
April 21, 1961

It is evident that many of our present day editors still go by thumb of rulebook on what has preceded them. The sanctuary of the rule means nothing to the pure creator. There is an excuse for poor creation if we are dithered by camouflage or wine come down through staring eyes, but there isn't any excuse for a creation crippled by directives of school and fashion, or the valetudinarian prayer book that says: form, form, form!! put it in a cage!

Let's allow ourselves space and error, hysteria and grief. Let's not round the edge until we have a ball that rolls neatly away like a trick. Things happen—the priest is shot in the john; hornets blow heroin without arrest; they take down your number; your wife runs off with an idiot who's never read Kafka; the crushed cat, its guts

41

glueing its skull to the pavement, is passed by traffic for hours; flowers grow in the smoke; children die at 9 and 97; flies are smashed from screens . . . the history of *form* is evident. I am the last to say we can start with zero, but let's get out of 8 or 9 and upward into 11. We may repeat—as we have been doing—about what is true, and have, I suppose, been doing it quite well. But I would like to see us scream a little more hysterically—if we are men enough— about the untrue also and the unformed and the never-to-be-formed. Really, we must let the candle burn—pour gasoline on it if necessary. The sense of the ordinary is always ordinary, but there are screams from windows too . . . an artistic hysteria engendered out of breathing in the necropolis . . . sometimes when the music stops and leaves us 4 walls of rubber or glass or stone, or worse—no walls at all—poor and freezing in the Atlanta of the heart. To concentrate on form and logic, "the turning of the phrase" seems imbecility in the midst of the madness.

I can not tell you how much the careful boys rip me naked with their planned and worked-over creations. Creation is our gift and we are ill with it. It has sloshed about my bones and awakened me to stare at 5 a.m. walls. And musing leads to madness like a dog with a rag doll in an empty house. Look, says a voice, into and beyond terror—Cape Canaveral, Cape Canaveral has nothing on us. hell, jack, this is wise-time: we must insist on camouflage, they taught us that—gods coughed alive through the indistinct smoke of verse. Look, says another voice, we must carve from fresh marble . . . What does it matter, says a third, what does it matter? the light yellow mamas are gone, the garter high on the leg; the charm of 18 is 80, and the kisses—snakes darting liquid silver— the kisses have stopped. no man lives the magic long . . . until one morning at 5 a.m. it catches you; you light a fire, pour a hasty drink as the psyche crawls like a mouse in an empty pantry. if you were Greco or even a watersnake, something could be done.

another drink. well, rub your hands and prove that you are alive. seriousness will not do. walk the floor.

this is the gift, this is the gift . . .

Certainly the charm in dying lies in the fact that nothing is lost.

[To Hilda Doolittle]
June 29, 1961

Have heard from Sheri M. that you are very ill. You are almost a legend with most of us. Have read your latest collected poems (Evergreen). I hope I will not sound foolish in wishing you well, and writing again.

Love,

[To Jon Webb]
Late July 1961

[. . .] Heard some of my poems read on the radio the other night. I wouldn't have even known, but [Jory] Sherman who keeps up with such told me over the phone, so I got drunk and listened. Very odd to hear own words coming back through speaker of radio that has told you news reports, freeway jams, played Beethoven and professional football games. One poem, the first of 15 was the roses poem in *Outsider*. Also read parts of my letters regarding editors and poetry readings and critics or something like that, and had audience, at times, laughing, as did a couple of the poems, so I did not feel so bad, but when I got up to get another beer I stepped on a 3 inch piece of glass on the floor (my place a mess) and glass went straight up into heel, and I yanked it out and bled for a couple of hours. I limped around for a week and then one day woke up covered with sweat, burning hot, vomiting . . . for a while, thought it was a hangover, but after a while decided it was not, and drove down Hollywood Blvd. to some Dr. Landers and got a shot. Got back, opened a beer, and immediately stepped on another piece of glass.

Jesus, I read in *Outsider* that the early [Henry] Miller made carbons of his work and shipped it to people. To me, this is inconceivable, but suppose Miller thot there weren't any openings for him and that he had to make his own openings. I suppose each man attacks it differently. Although I see where Grove issued his *Tropic,* and now that it is a safe thing, it is falling pretty flat in most quarters. Also note that *Life* mag and others gave it to Hem. pretty good in the ass. Which he deserved, having pretty much sold out after his early works, which I always knew but which I never heard anybody say until after his suicide. Why did they wait?

Faulkner is, in essence, much like Hem. The public has swallowed him with one big gulp and the critics, having something a little more subtle, feel safe and egg them on, but a lot of Faulkner's pure shit, but it's clever shit, cleverly dressed, and when he goes they will have trouble rubbing him out because they don't quite understand him, and not understanding him, the dull and vacant parts, the mass of italics, they will think this to mean genius.

[To John William Corrington]
Late August 1961

[. . .] As you know, I am very sloppy. I don't keep carbons. Stuff that's out and accepted I have no copies of. Stuff that's out and not coming back I have no copies of. Sometimes I find a piece of paper with something written on it, or a typewritten paper but I don't know if it's accepted or if I ever sent it out. I've even lost a sheet of paper I used to keep that told me where I had sent some poems or where some had been accepted, but what the titles of the poems were, I didn't know. And now I've lost the piece of paper. I had a wife once [Barbara Fry] who really amazed me. She'd write a poem and send it out, write down the name of the poem, date, where sent . . . She had a large bookkeeping book, a beautiful thing, and in it she had a list of magazines, and the magazine list crossed screw-wise or blue lines over orange or something and she made little asterisk **** that webbed it all together. It was one hell of a beautiful thing. She could run the same poem down thru 20 or 30 magazines just by ****************** ********** and never send to the same mag twice, hurrah. She had a book for me but I drew dirty pictures and things in mine. And when she wrought a poem, each one she wrote wd be typed again on special paper and then pasted in a notebook (with date). I could use a little of this moxie but really I think it would make me feel a little too much like I was selling form-fit bras from door to door.

1962

[To John William Corrington]
April 1962

[. . .] Fry once egged me on to make a bunch of cartoons with captions, the joke bit, and I stayed up all night, drinking and making these cartoons, laughing at my own madness. There were so many of them by morning that I couldn't get them in an envelope, none large enough, so I made a big thing out of cardboard, and mailed it to either the *New Yorker* or *Esquire,* putting another cardboard thing inside with proper postage. Well, hell, they could prob. see I was either amateur or mad. It never came back. I wrote about my 45 cartoons and they never came back. "No such item rec. from you," wrote back some editor. But sitting in a barbershop a couple of months later I came across one of my jokes in some mag, I believe *Man,* showing a guy, a jock whipping a horse with one of those round balls with spikes on the end of a chain, and one guy along the rail is telling another, "He's a very rude boy but somehow effective." The words were changed just a little and the drawing a little, but it sure seemed just like mine. Well, hell, you can imagine anything if you want to imagine anything. But I don't know, I wasn't even looking, I usually don't even look into magazines or maybe I do but don't realize it, but I kept popping across my same ideas and drawings just altered a touch; it was all too close, all too much the same to be anything

46

but mine, only I felt that mine were better executed, and I do not mean killed, they killed that. And when I came across one of my largest no-caption drawings (I mean, the idea of it, it was not my drawing) upon the FRONT COVER OF THE *NEW YORKER*, then, I knew I'd had it—it was the same damn thing: a large lake on a moonlit night with all these dozens of canoes filled with male and female, and in each the male was playing a guitar and serenading his female—except in one boat right in the center of the lake was this guy standing up in his canoe and blowing this very huge horn. I forgot whether I put a broad in his canoe or not, I prob. did, but now as I am older I see it would have given an extra laugh to leave the gash out. Anyhow, it was all wasted and I didn't cartoon no more until Ben Tibbs kinda fucked up on what was supposed to be a cover for *Longshot Pomes* and I told [Carl] Larsen jesus I think I can do better. What I mean is, like with the cartoons, the novel, I don't know the mechanics of doing and I do not want to waste a lot of words doing everything backwards that some sycophant will twist and turn to his own use. I thought the Art world and things like that would be clean. That's shit. There are more evil and unscrupulous octopus people in the Art world than you'll find in any business house because in a business house the guy's minnow imagination is just on getting a bigger house and a bigger car and an extra whore but usually the drive does not come from some twisted inside that cries for RECOGNITION OF SELF beyond all decency and straightness, no matter how it's gotten. That's why some of these editors are such damn buggers: they can't carve it themselves so they try to associate themselves with those who hack and carve at a little clean marble . . . that's why a lot of them won't answer letters of inquiry about submitted work: all the lights within them have fucked themselves to pieces and out.

I went to nightschool once, on Fry's insistence, took what

you call it? commercial Art. This guy who taught worked for some outfit that did comm. art and taught school at night. We'd bring our work to class and he'd line it along the blackboard, and one time just before the Christmas season he said, "Now my company has to do a sign for the TEXACO gas stations, and I want you to make this your problem. Give us something for a xmas ad." Well, the time came around and he was passing along the board looking at the drawings until he came to mine, and with a great fury and anger he turned to the class and roared: "WHO DID THIS ONE???!!!" "I did," I admitted, "I thought the TEXACO star, the idea of having the TEXACO star and emblem at the top of the tree was a good one." "No Christmas trees, please. This is no good. I want you to make me another drawing." He walked on.

A couple of weeks later he stood before the class. "Well, my company and the TEXACO executives have chosen our Christmas ad." And he held it up. And as he did so, just a moment after he did so, I saw his eyes search me out. You know what he held up: A Christmas tree with a TEXACO emblem star at the top, only they had put a little service station man inside the tree . . . I didn't say anything. I could have made him look bad. But I am not for arguing, bitching. I felt that he knew that I knew and that was sufficient. I dropped out of class and got drunk. Later, during the Xmas season, when we'd pass a Texaco station I'd tell Fry, "Look, baby, my drawing . . . aren't you proud of me?"

what I mean is if I wrote this novel on toilet paper somebody wd wipe his ass on it. I wrote the Ape thing as a short story some 15 years ago or so and IT NEVER CAME BACK EITHER. and no carbons. but I doubt John Collier copied it. He prob. has more talent than I and needn't do such things. The ape story has done me good, though; I usually tell it to ladies in bed after everything else has been done and we are more or less relaxed. Fry thought the telling was wonderful, and another lady cried, "oh, I'm going to cry, I'm going to cry, it was so sad and beautiful." and she cried. I guess the reason it didn't come back (the story) was that I was broke and drinking at the time and was hand-printing my stuff in ink. I finally got so that I could print faster than I could write in longhand and whenever I wrote something down I printed it and people would say, "What the hell's wrong with you? Don't you know how to write?" I can't answer that. I don't know if I can write or not. But I'm sure laying on the bologna tonight . . . blue true bologna and a bellyfull.

———————

This Toilet Paper Review *predates the version published in* Screams from the Balcony *(1993).*

[To John William Corrington]
Late April 1962

I got an idea, Willie. Let's you and I put out an issue. Call it the *The Toilet Paper Review*. We won't even need a duplicator. I will just get a roll and type it up in this typewriter. We will, just you and I, run all our old poems we can't get rid of in *The Toilet Paper Review*. One copy to *Trace,* one copy to God, one copy for Sherman and one for Sherman's whore who can take it. Anywhere. Anyhow.

The Toilet Paper Review
Edited by William Corrington and Charles Bukowski
Vol. I, #I
      if ya wanna look at television
      we don't give a shit.

"I Kneel"
By William Corrington

these legs need to run
but I kneel
before female flowers—
catch the scent of forgetfulness
and grab it,
sure,
and evenings
hours of evenings
grey-headed evenings
nod
and afterwards

"Sculpture"
By Charles Bukowski

Harry, the habit, and then we made
this face, and then out of the Face
came: fish, elms, butternut candy,
and we went outside
and we went outside
and we—needle off, or
break the tape, I can't stand
it anymore,
I walked 18 blocks,
came back, and the face
had grown to the size of the room
and I knew it was true:
I was mad.

"The Alley That Waits Us"
By William Corrington

I guess we must go on,
loss after loss,
we must go on,
until the final loss,
say in some alley,
blood running down like a
necktie ha ha, we are
tricked and slapped to death,
bargained out of any gain,
any love, any rest,
hands to walls, waa waaa!,
traffic (grr!!) going by,
filthy lovers making filthy
lover's vows, fish sick fish
going out with the tide
waa waaa!! mah head a
falling now, we are almost
into the black dream,
never to be genius now,
sun brings tulips, rain brings
worms, God brings genius
and disposes genius tulip
worm so things begin again
new things forever
tiresome tiresome to think
body flat now
az small ratz run to my shoes
run off again
and I am seen by a small boy
and he too

runs runs
but they will catch him
like the tulips
like Poppa
like Belmonte
like large stones that break
into sand
that cuts where there is blood,
loss after loss
wherever we
are.

(and we still don't give a shit whether u look at T.V. or not.
We need subscribers. Please help.)

[To John William Corrington]
May 1962

[. . .] I received a letter from some woman today. She gives me Nietzsche: "what we do is never understood, but only praised and blamed." And then she says, "This must be what you meant when you spoke of the bad influence of praise in your letter. But, think—to be praised AND to be understood! There, my Friend, is the only type of practical paradise for the writer or the painter or the composer . . ." "Very true—the artist must certainly go from one creation to the next, but none of them are entire new beginnings—nothing ever really has a new beginning. One creation evolves from another. One purpose turns into ten thousand others. When you find an inspired thought, in your head, surely you can not believe it is breathlessly new? It came from centuries of submerged creations of ideas. But I do not mean to get started on a long dragged out 'essay' . . ."

Well, thank Christ for that.

what a bunch of fucking preconceptions, and what a dismal harnessed outlook. These intelligent people jaggle my nuts. Each beginning to me (TO ME!!!) is a NEW BEGINNING. God yas. How else do I know whether I am dead or not? what wiggles. what gives. the cunts. I must see the cunts. Each flower is a new flower. The others are dead. Good they were, but dead. I know that when I look at a bridge or a building that this thing is a COMPILATION of so-called knowledge. So fuck a horse. When I write a poem, I add a bolt, a red-nosed bolt with a sour middle and a bloody ass. Or maybe—better yet—I TAKE OUT A BOLT. But I don't wanna be hamstrung with these purposeful essays. If this bitch wants to come down and ride the springs with me, o.k. Otherwise, my thoughts are not "inspired."

Somebody says they saw Mailer on T.V. Says very neurotic and can't finish a sentence. Mailer may not be much but what has this got to do with writing. If a person is very N. and cannot finish a sentence chances are he will be a better writer than the reversal. What's wrong? Everybody sees backwards. [. . .]

I like your letters better than the Henry Miller letters. The Millers seem rather bitchy and cloying as if he were trying to make Walter L[owenfels] climb somewhere. And then this Huxley thing. H. imitates M. just a little too much, just a little too hard. Almost as if Miller thought Huxley were almost good and he had to stamp on him a little to push him down. Huxley shouldn't bother you if you take Huxley as Huxley, an over-read over-educated almost-brilliant limey who forgot where the blood was. But an entertaining writer. It's like going to a stage play that has dropped in from Broadway after a 13 day run. You don't expect Shakespeare. So why the spears?

[To Jon Webb]
September 14, 1962

I don't know how to write a "letter of acceptance." I can write letters of resignation, or a letter like this:

Baby:
  I know it's not any good anymore. I've been walking around thinking about it while you are at work. I am finishing the pint. Found ten dollars in the dresser and am leaving. I leave behind for you my copy of Jeno Barcsay's Anatomy for the Artist *and the 2* Milton Cross' Encyclopedia of the Great Composers. *Take care of the dog. Christ, how I loved that hound!*
  yrs.,
  Bubu . . .

Then I hope this Award is not to keep the blade from my throat, although it might well do that. Yet better men than I have left their blood in the dry dahlias. I just hope I can slam out some more things that will let in a little more light on myself and everything else.

This, of course, is the purpose of the Artist besides trying to keep from going mad. All in all, no matter how pessimistic, analytical or mathematical we get about the thing, I can't help thinking that there is nobleness in the battle, that death has been a little adjusted to, that, in our weeping and our laughter and our rage we have made some indentation, some road, something to *hang onto* besides our love in the love bed, besides flakes of night and tombstones. [. . .]

I am still in fog on this Award business and walk around tasting it on the end of my tongue. There is a lot of child in me. If you decide to go ahead with it and want to use letters or parts of letters, fine. I think the letter itself is important as a form, just as the poem-form, and it has a way of saying that the poem-form does not, and also the other way around. This is an odd day. I almost feel good. [. . .]

The only thing you know, Jon, is what I know: that art is art and names are secondary. We are not politicians of the literary scene. Black Mountain, New Critique, *Folder*, West Coast, East Coast, G. with A., L with X, we do not know who is sleeping with shitwho and we don't care. Why do these jackoffs form in circles? Why do they complain? Fucking bunch of tit and cocksuckers trying to sweep out every voice but their own. This is only natural. Survival. But who wants to survive as a cocksucker except those who brag about it? As you know, I have done some editing myself and know the terrific pressures. You print me and I'll print you. I am a friend of J.B.'s (and I don't mean MacLeish's *J.B.*). Everybody is afraid of *Trace*. [James Boyer] May gets published in half or 3/4's of the mags in this country, not because his poems are good but because he is the editor of *Trace*. This is wrong. Sure. And there are other wrongs that creep into the scene like slime. Art is Art and Art should be its own hammer.

Do you think I am really going mad? Why do I write such a long letter? Something is oozing out here.

Is this the way it goes when you carve poems? Does everything come down? your job, your life, your wife, your country, your mind, everything but your love and the sound of the word, the carving, the carving, carving, carving. . . . o my god yes

I know how Van Gogh felt

I wonder if he carried shit and blood in his pants
and painted on elephants ears?

How can these boys stand a chance, these 4-f hairy poets and
  practitioners
    when they drink goat's milk, punch clocks,
      raise families, move to Glendale, vote for Nixon,
    wax their cars, bury grandma, take vitamins,
  how can they make it. haw how can they make it????
        standing *outside* the fire?

You tell me, please, if you can play it safe and still sing the
madman's beautiful song? No. I'll tell you. It's impossible. Then . . .
there is the other type, just as sickening, who *play* the Artist and
don't have the Art. Beards. Mary. Sandals. Jazz. Tea. H. Coffee-
shops. Homo-bit. Nirvana on a shoestring. Poetry readings. Poetry
clubs. Awk, I must stop. I am sick enough of everything.

---

*Bukowski is responding to a letter by Felix Stefanile, written in reac-
tion to Bukowski being named "Outsider of the Year" by* The Outsider
editors.

[To Jon Webb]
Late October 1962

[. . .] On the Stefanile; people like Felix are puzzled. They
have all these concepts and pre-concepts of what poetry *should* be.
Mostly they are still in the 19th century. If a poem doesn't look like
Lord Byron, then you've got crackers in your bed. The politicians
and newspapers talk a lot about freedom but the moment you begin
to apply any, either in Life or in the Art-form, you are in for a cell,
ridicule or misunderstanding. I sometimes think when I put that
sheet of white paper in the typer . . . you will soon be dead, we will

56

all soon be dead. Now it may not be too bad being dead but while you're living it might be best to live from the source stuck inside of you, and if you're honest enough you might end up in the drunk-tank 15 or 20 times and lose a few jobs and a wife or 2 or maybe slug somebody in the streets and sleep on a park bench now and then; and if you come to the poem, you are not going to worry too much about writing like Keats, Swinburne, Shelley; or acting like Frost. You are not going to worry about spondees, counts, or if the endings rhyme. You want to get it down, hard or crude or otherwise—any way you can truly send it through. I don't think that this means that I "cavort in left-field" . . . "performing with both hands" and at the top of my voice, as Mr. S. puts it, "waving his poems like a flag." This rather infers a sense of being heard at any cost. This infers bad art for the sake of fame. This infers somewhat the stage-play and the fake. But these charges have gone on down through the centuries in all the Arts—and they continue now in painting, music, sculpture, the novel. The mass, both the actual mass and the Artistic mass (in the sense of large practicing numbers only) are always far behind, practicing safety not only in the material and economic life but in the life of the so-called soul. If you wear a straw hat in December you are dead. If you write a poem that escapes the mass-hypnosis of 19th century slick-soft poesy they think that you write badly because you do not sound right. They want to hear what they have always heard. But they forget that it takes 5 or 6 good men every century to push the thing ahead out of staleness and death. I am not saying that *I* am one of these men but I am sure as hell saying I am *not* one of the others. Which leaves me hanging—OUTSIDE.

Well, Jon, I'd say run the thing by Stefanile if you find the space. It is a viewpoint. And I'd much rather be described as a brick-layer or pugilist than as a poet. So it's all not so bad.

57

[To the editors of *Coastlines*]
Late 1962

Biog.? I am insane and old and driveling, smoke like the forests of hell, but feel better all the time, that is—worse and better. And when I sit down to the typer it is like carving tits on a cow—a great big thing. Then too, I realize I gotta run in the Latin, and the poise, and the snob and the Pound and the Shake[speare], and hello hello hell—anything that makes the thing run, hurrah! But I am thin as a fake, so I often write a bad poem written mostly by myself rather than a good poem written mostly by somebody else. Though, of course, I cannot swear by this. Examination and reexamination. Why try? Those who sit constantly in symphony halls adore creation but cannot create. I go to the racetrack where they also have bars. All hail the mad gods who have created these fine spinning things.

1963

[To John William Corrington]
January 20, 1963

[. . .] Now that you are C[harles] P[ercy] Snow and Lion[el] Trill and T. S. and the vulgate desires of the frustrate hair-skewers will be listed, I had better stay on your best side, yr good side, God-side, where I imagine your .357 is tucked while you dance the saraband. All this quite interesting, for you are a hell of a lot better poet than you are a critic, and while you are talking about other people, other people should be reading you, you are steaming up like a truckload of dry ice filled on the San Berdo Freeway. Anyhow, that will take care of itself . . . On [Robert] Creeley, yes, it is more or less a trick; the poetry (his) is so white and dry and empty they figure, well, yes, Christ, I guess it is really something because there is nothing there and this man must BE so VURY SUBTLE AND INTEELIGENT, christ ya, because it appears I don't understan wha he doin. It's like a game of chess played in a sunny room with the rent paid ten years in advance, and nobody knows the winner because the winner makes the rules and doesn't try very hard. If you wake up in a back alley with your shirt torn and you rise along the bricks, the cold wind coming in between your knees and your balls, and you've got a mouthful of blood and a couple of knots on your head, and when you reach in your pocket, the rear one, and you get that empty feeling of hand upon ass, wallet gone, all 500 bucks, driver's license, phone number of Jesus, you aren't a poet, you are just caught out of place and you don't know how to act. When the bitch with big tits laughed at all your jokes youse shoulda jammed the glass right up her snatcher. The Creeleys will never know death; even when it arrives they will think it is for somebody else. [Gregory] Corso at least thinks about Death. *And* Corso. If his name were Hamacheck he never would have become known. The world of Art is like a bunch of fucking ivy growing everywhere. It's all on the rain and the luck and where the building is and who walks by and what yr doing, like what ivy are you crawling with or sleeping with or what Black Mountain crew, or god, I must stop, I am sick.

[To John William Corrington]
March 9, 1963

[. . .] I don't think there is such a thing as *Outsider* #3. I feel like I did when I was a kid in high school, when they made me sit in a phone booth while I waited to see the principal, a distinguished-looking fuck, grey-haired, long-haired, pince-nez, victorian voice, and he dressed me down after keeping me in that booth for an hour waiting with a copy of the *Ladies Home Journal*. I forgot what I did; it seemed something like murder. A couple of years later I read where they got the old boy for misappropriation of funds. Anyhow, with *Outsider* 3, now, I am sitting in the phone booth, waiting. You can't blame me for getting edgy. It wasn't over 8 months ago that I was sitting on the damned cliff's edge testing razorblades with the edge of my thumb.

Corrington wrote "Charles Bukowski: Three Poems," published in The Outsider *3, as well as "Charles Bukowski at Midflight," an introduction to Bukowski's* It Catches My Heart in Its Hands *(1963).*

[To John William Corrington]
March 19, 1963

Got *The Outsider* number 3, and fantoccini grapes and hail!!!—thair on cover I appear, torturer of rats and infants and old ladies, and the honor is heavy, almost too heavy to bear, so you know, I did the easy thing, I got drunk, but really the thing has yet to take the shape of reality, and I know this kind of talk gets tiresome, but they can never ever really again strike me down because this thing was done by these 2 people in the hardest sort of way, and no wonder they are interested in OUTSIDERS, for can't you see, that's what THEY are? And most pleasing of all, they did not mutilate me or freak me up, but let it just fall the way it is. This is what happens when editors have SOULS, and after battling and hating editors all my life, it has to come to this: an almost awe of the workmanship, manner and miracle of these 2 people—not because they put me on a cover, printed some letters etc.; but in the grand manner, they did it so god damned well that neither pride nor honor is lost. I am very aware that my mind will eventually go soft with drink and age—if I live—but nothing outside of death will ever quite bear this time away from me. All the walls and whores and days and nights of hell did not earn this for me. I was lucky. And since I have been . . . unlucky . . . I take and accept this #3, ages of my life gone, almost, everything gone, but this.

I can't get over about how well they did it. They must understand more about me than I understand about myself.

And now, on top of everything, I get these notes from Jon, blue slips of paper etc.: "We will soon be into the book . . . Corrington coming down, busy, busy, busy . . ."

A book on top of all this seems almost impossible, but unless you think I grow soft—joy does seep through here—understand, that certain allowance with 2 or 3 people does not mean that I grow soft (yet?) in the head. I'm not like Frost: he had a lover's quarrel with the world and he won; I had a fighter's fight with the world and I lost. I intend to keep losing but I doubt that I intend to quit fighting. There is a difference and if I speak well of 2 or 3 people, it is done because the speaking breaks through and I am at a loss to guard it, do not want to. [. . .]

What I mean, Willie iz: you did good article on my 3 poems, and I hope you do intro for book, you are one of the luckiest things that has happened to me outside of Jane and a horse that paid me $222.60, or something like that for a deuce 2 or 3 years back. Putting it lightly. Jane is dead. The horse is prob. dead. You are here. I pray. You, like Jon and Louise, did me great honor, and knowing this is meant . . . without pressure, coercion . . . meant because it was only meaning to you, I take it gently and with warmth, you South bastard, and "The Tragedy of the Leaves" I remember (as a poem) the best of them all. "Old Man, Dead in a Room" may yet hold true. If I wrote my own epitaph (which is what I meant it to be), it was because sometime ahead of time I could see this truly becoming so, and I still hold to this. Fame or immortality will not be mine. Actually, I do not want it. I mean, it is grissly girly grizzly gouchey what??? He, who fucks wants to stick his cock of self into that long black dawn with INTENT must truly have something wrong with himself, or dirt under his fingernails.

[To Edward van Aelstyn]
March 31, 1963

Got your o.k. on the 2 poems "A Drawer of Fish" and "Breakthrough."

About *Outsider* #3, Webb does it the hard way, of course, and pretty much alone, so that when he comes across some precious group with staff and walking shorts gathered upon a North Carolina mountaintop (or wherever the Black Mountain School originated), it brings a boil to the mind (this something already settled before we—the readers—get to it) and this time it exploded. Of course, all through the history of the Arts—painting, music, lit., these schools have existed, sometimes because the individual artist was too weak to fail alone (it's much easier to succeed alone), or other times because groups of artists were *made* into schools by the critics; but hell, you know all this. What I would like to point out, however, is that Webb has given Creeley space and has given space to Creeleyites on the seeming weakness or strength of their work alone; but the objection that Webb voices is that they are unable to work alone, and there is a network of defense that is wrought up whenever (it seems) one of the holy members are criticized.

My criticism of Creeley is far more (seemingly) vicious: I don't think he can write. I have no doubt that he thinks the same of me.

There is only one thing or 2 an artist can do: go on writing or stop writing. Sometimes he goes on and stops at the same time. Eventually, of course, the Impartial Critic gets us all and we stop pretty damned good.

I am glad you think of guarding the soul, this has been quite forgotten by many or is regarded as Romantic Rubbish of a more unimplemented past when it appeared that we did not know as much about ourselves as we do now. But the basics remain the same: if you roll in shit long enough you are going to look like it. The only thing we've got to do is find out what it is so we won't roll in it. I would hate as much to teach a class in Freshman English as I would to turn bolts in a factory. Each is damning enough. And when you are through with that part, the leisure we have left waits upon us. This is the big trick to turn. And many times, no matter how well you turn the trick, the other part—turning the bolt, teaching Freshman English, eats you away. Some artists (more so in the past, I feel, than in the present) get more leisure by not working and therefore starving in order to gain Time, but this too often contains a trap with teeth: suicide or madness. I can now write better, I think, on a full stomach, but maybe it is because I remember all the years it was empty and that it will, most probably, be that way again. Saving the soul depends upon what you do—and not the obvious things—and what and how much you have to begin with and how much you might possibly even *gain* along the way. There are professional soul-savers, intellectuals, who go by standard formula and therefore are saved in only a standard sort of way—which is like not being saved at all. The few people I know sometimes ask me, "Why do you drink and go to the race track?" It would make far more sense to them if I stayed inside for a month and stared at the walls. What they do not realize is that I have already done this. What they do not realize is that if I do not hear the hard tack and rattle of words in my gut, I am done, and so I go where this helps it occur (the bottle) (the crowd), so far. Later, maybe, I won't care.

This writing the poem often brings strange ladies to the door, knocking, and they think the poem means love, so I have to give them love, and that may be—haha!—what's left of the soul . . . going there. I guess part of it is down around the belly. The last one just left this afternoon after 4 days and nights, and I sit down to write you this thing upon . . . aesthetics, and the Black Mountain School, and that I got your o.k. on the 2 poems, and sure, I can use the check too. It has been a warm afternoon and a long one, in a way, the eyes all splotched with love . . . peeking at me from between the rungs of the bed as I read the race results . . . god damn, god damn, is this living? Is this the way it's done? With 9 bottles of beer and 16 cigarettes left, on the last night of March in 1963, Cuba and the Berlin Wall, and these walls here cracking, me cracking, a brittle 42 years wasted . . . van, van, the Beast is not Death. . . .

Corrington published "Charles Bukowski and the Savage Surfaces," in Northwest Review *in 1963. The lines Bukowski quotes almost verbatim below belong to "Westron Wynde," which is believed to be a fragment of medieval poetry.*

[To John William Corrington]
May 1, 1963

red flags draped all over; red shorts anyhow . . . 3 rejected poems back from [Sergio] Mondragón, very curt. all now normal and I see through my 2 front eyes.

—on poetry of the surfaces, I am glad I am savage as accused, glad not to belong, and you understand this, of course, because you seem to see pretty well beyond the obvious. I've spent my hours in the library with Schope[nhauer] and Ari[stotle] and Plato and the rest, but when some kind of teeth are digging into you it doesn't set for calmness and meditation. Twice today at the track I had people walk up to me, the first asked: "Hey, didn't you once work in a Studebaker factory?" The other guy was worse; he said: "Tell

65

me, didn't you once drive a bread wagon?" I haven't done either of these things but I have done many things of this sort that have sort of slugged my head into frogshape undazzle, and they figure I've had it, which I have had, only they are thinking in terms of some other poor fuck who's had it. Fine and lacy poetry & thoughts are for those who have time for them. God's pretty far away from me, maybe inside a beerbottle somewhere, and sure I'm crude, they've made me crude, and in another sense I am crude because I want to work things down to where they are—that is, the knife going in, or staring at a whore's asshole, that's where the work is going on, and I don't want to be fooled too much and I don't want to fool anybody else. Let's say, even subconsciously, that this self of mine is thinking in terms of CENTURIES, which is pretty tough stuff. A lot of my playing dumb or crude or boorish is done to *eliminate* horseshit. Maybe I figure that this stuff is going to smell pretty bad if I say a lot of things I think *might* be true in conjecture. I think I could fool the boys. I think I could come on pretty heavy. I can toss vocabulary like torn-up mutual tickets, but I think eventually the words that will be saved are the small stone-like words that are said and meant. When men really mean something they don't say it in 14 letter words. Ask any woman. They know. I keep remembering a poem I read with a lot of other poems quite some centuries old, quite old, and it's true that when you go back far enough things become simple and clear and good because maybe that's what was saved, maybe that's all the years could stand, or maybe they were better men then, maybe all that heavy false creamy 18th and 19th century part was a reaction to truth, men get tired of truth just as they get tired of evil, but who knows—anyhow, in all these aged poems there was one went something like this, bill:

> oh god
> to have my love in my arms

and back in my bed
again!

that's crude. I like it.

Then I've had people say, "Why do you go to the racetrack?
Why do you drink? This is destruction." Hell yes, it's destruction.
So was working for 17$ a week in New Orleans destruction. So were
the piles of white bodies, old ankles and shinbones and shit strung
through the sheets of L.A. County General Hospital . . . the dead
waiting to die . . . the old sucking at the mad air with nothing but
walls and silence and a county grave, like a garbage pit, waiting.
They think I don't give a damn, they think I don't feel because my
face is done and my eyes are poked out and I stand there with a
drink, looking at the racing form. *They* feel in such a NICE way, the
fuckers, the pricks, the slimy smiling lemon-sucking turd-droppers,
they feel, sure, the CORRECT WAY, only there isn't any correct
way, and they'll know it . . . some night, some morning, or maybe
some day on a freeway, the last rumble of glass and steel and blad-
der in the rose-growing sunlight. They can take their ivy and their
spondees and stick them up their ass . . . if something is not already
up there.

Besides, it pays to be crude, buddy, it PAYS. When these
women who have read my poetry knock on my door and I ask them
in and pour them a drink, and we talk about Brahms or Corrington
or Flash Gordon, they know all along that it is GOING TO HAPPEN,
and that makes the talk nice

    because pretty soon the bastard is just going
        to walk over and grab me
    and get started
            because he's been around
                he's CRUDE

And so, since they expect it, I do it, and this gets a lot of barriers and small-talk out of the way fast. Women like bulls, children, apes. The pretty boys and the expounders upon the universe don't stand a chance. They end up jacking-off in the closet.

There's a guy down at work, he says, "I recite Shakespeare to them."

He's still a virgin. They know he's scared. Well, we're all scared but we go ahead.

[To Marvin Malone]
August 5, 1963

Well, I walked upstairs with the heavy envelope, thinking, well they are prob. still all in here, it's tough like sending elephants through mud, but I opened the thing and found you had taken ELEVEN, which is a lot no matter how many I had sent. I don't know much about the ratings you gave the remainder; I am not addicted to reading my stuff after writing it. It's like hanging onto faded flowers. They say Li Po burned his and sailed them down the river, but I figure in his case he was a pretty good self-critic and that he burned only the bad ones; then when the prince came up and asked for some stuff he plucked the good ones from close to his belly—down by the painting of the Manchurian doll with blue eyes. [. . .]

I hope when your co-editor gets back into town he is feeling good . . . Writing is a damn funny game. Rejection helps because it makes you write better; acceptance helps because it keeps you writing. I will be 43 years old in 11 days. It seems o.k. to write poetry at 23 but when you're going at it at 43 you've got to figure there's a little something twisted in your head, but that's o.k.—

another smoke, another drink, another woman in your bed, and the sidewalks are still there and the worms and the flies and the sun; and it's a man's own business if he'd rather fiddle with a poem than invest in real estate, and eleven poems are good, glad you found so many. The curtains wave like a flag over my country and the beer is tall.

1964

[To Jack Conroy]
May 1, 1964

My thanks for *The Disinherited*, which I have now read and which lays to my right as I type this, and I am listening to Tch[aikovsky]'s 6th. symphony and drinking a small beer; tired; bet quarter horses today, and it's win soon, or decay or knife-sharpening, all very depressive—but the book, the book, yes, it went well, and what interested me was that it showed how it was mostly for people like me and you and people we knew and know; how it was, and for my money, how it still is. It's hell to be poor, that's no secret; it's hell to be sick without money, hungry without money; it's hell to be sick and hungry forever down to the last day. The God-forsaken jobs which most of us must hold; the God-forsaken jobs which most of us must *hunt* for, beg for; the God-forsaken jobs which we hate with all our tiring spirit and must still engage in . . . my god, the alcoholics, the poets, the suicides, the addicts, the madmen all this vomits up! I do not understand why we must live in such horrible, dreary and obviously abject fashion in a century where a civilization has devised through all its energy the force large enough to kill us all. I think that if it is possible to destroy life completely then, by Christ, it is also possible to allow life to live completely. And I mean, *completely;* I don't mean just enough to allow our millionaires and statesmen a chance to escape to some

70

planet after they've fucked up the works here . . . But I'm getting away from your book, and it's a good time for reissue because the same hellish jobs are still there, the same discarding of the old, the same sense of hardness that makes an unemployed man a social outcast without an excuse, without a voice, without a chance. I know about the almost-impossibility of survival. I worked for $17 a week in Louisiana and was fired when I asked for a 2 dollar a week raise. This was in 1941. I've worked in slaughterhouses, washed dishes; worked in a fluorescent light factory; hung posters in New York subways, scrubbed freightcars and washed passenger trains in the railroad yards; been a stock boy, a shipping clerk, a mailman, a bum, a gas station attendant, coconut man in a cake factory, a truck driver, a foreman in a book-distributing warehouse, a carrier of bottles of blood and a rubber tube squeezer for the Red Cross; crapshooter, horseplayer, madman, fool, god, I can't remember them all, but reading your book a lot of it came back to me. I used to sign up for track gangs in order to travel about the country. I once went from New Orleans to Los Angeles this way; another time from L.A. to Sacramento. They'd give us cold cans of food which we had to bust open against the backs of seats or other places because there were no can openers. These cold rotten cans were charged against our account to be taken out of our first paychecks, plus, I suppose, travel expenses. I don't know—I was always leaping off. So were others. But those who hung on I understand worked quite a period for nothing. There was always somebody with a bottle and a pair of dice and we took our food tickets, one time, which were good in a place on Main street L.A. and got drunk on beer there along with 6 or 7 others and we shook hands and parted. Balls, this is not your book I am talking about, but I do want you to know I understood much of it, and thanks again for sending it along. I'm not saying you're Jack London; I'm saying you're Jack Conroy, which is o.k.

[To Walter Lowenfels]
May 1, 1964

[. . .] I don't know who Juvenal is; when I put down *The Daily Racing Form* my eyes hurt.

I am looking out the window at a hill sliced in half and there are 7 cans of beer in my icebox. Life is good.

Writing is like most writers think fucking is: just when they start thinking they are doing it pretty good they stop doing it altogether.

I hope to go a few more rounds but I know that thing is waiting there, that thing that tears most of us apart long before we're dead, that tiger, that whore, that black cloth, that toenail.

christ be with you, and the dook, and the pink kite a boy is sailing 2 blocks North.

I am going for a walk.

[To Harold Norse]
May 12, 1964

[. . .] Yes, you're right: failure is the advantage and I mean the failure of not being held up phonepole high while you're working with the broad or the poem or the wax statue of Himmler. It's best to stay loose, work wild and easy and fail any way you want to. Once you polevault 17 feet they want 18 and it ends up you might break your leg trying. The mob must always be dismissed as something as insane as a river full of vomit. Once you put the mob in the wastebasket where it belongs you've got a chance to go a good ten and maybe get a split verdict. I do not speak of The Culture of Snobbery which is practiced by many of the rich and the fakirs and rope coilers and electricians and sports writers because they have an idea they have POWER. They are all dependent on the mob like the leaves hanging to the tree branch. What I mean is the kind of dependence that leaves you free to operate widely because you don't *need* a kiss on the cheek from the old lady next door, you don't need praiseology or to lecture before the Armenian Society of Pasadena writers. I mean, fuck that. More paper, more beer, more luck, loose bowels, an occasional piece of ass and good weather, who needs more? Rent, sure. Now I don't know what I'm talking about anymore. That's the danger of talking. You talk talk talk all wax and wallow and pretty soon you don't know what you are saying . . . I don't . . . that's why I feel much better when I am mostly quiet.

1965

Antin published a poem by Bukowski in some/thing *v. 2 no. 1 (1966), featuring Andy Warhol's art on the front cover.*

[To David Antin]
January 16, 1965

my thanks for copy of *some/thing* [v.] uno [no.] 2, some time back, and I had trouble with it, but I mostly have trouble with everything and so this isn't new, and so being Bing Crosby mouth, I look through your issue and find the same trouble as the ache of centuries—all too cute and clever, too intelligent and *dull*, tricky, major & excessive use of italics—I, for one, maybe only one—was very happy, well, maybe not very happy, but breathed more when Faulkner died, not that there was more room but that he would make them less dizzy. we are fucked enough, and tickled and tricked enough in our everyday lives. too much, surely. and I mean big CAPS too. you boys xlently drive the printer nuts. hand in balls. I have enclosed manu I have just written while in my usual state. why brag? I am drunk as often as possible and would use all sorts of other stuff except it's too hard to get and also penalty is extreme for getting caught and there are enough penalties upon my back like speriment serpents now wow and how, oh my. what I mean on the manu, isiz, please return if you can't use, I don't keep carbons as carbons make my pecker limp and I come right off of the typer.

very much I grate against use of poetic symbols to get the poetic state: viz—

as such

> green star ¾ ¾ //
>> erraiti
>> / I begged for
>> doorways entr/
>>> ance

I mean, let's stop fucking around and
begin talking.

Franklyn published a harsh review of Bukowski's Run with the Hunted *in* Grande Ronde Review *(1964).*

[To Mel Buffington]
Late April 1965

[. . .] Yes, I heard from [R. R.] Cuscaden on the fred franklyn thing, and Cuscaden seemed raped, outraged, finger-fucked with the below-the-belt method of criticism (Cuscaden put out *Run with the Hunted*). Anyway, from his letter, the Franklyn thing really got to him. I did not buy a copy to look up my burial and demise. let the dogs worry each other. I've got things to do like sleep, and pick hardened snot from my nostrils, and say like now—watch this thing dressed in grey pants and she has spider legs and yet an ass like a washtub, she walks past this window and my limp pecker twitches as bellies full of worms in paradise sing out of birds in this warm Los Angeles evening.

Run with the Hunted was some time ago, yet I'm glad I wrote the thing. I wonder what Freddie boy could do with *It Catches My Heart in Its Hands*, or like yesterday I got my first copy of *Crucifix in a Deathhand,* one of 3100 copies, new poems 1963–1965. Freddy's gonna have a big breakfast.

It appears that certain people think that poetry should be a certain way. For these, there will be nothing but troubled years. More and more people will come along to break their concepts. It's hard I know, like having somebody fuck your wife while you are at work, but life, as they say, goes on.

[To Steve Richmond]
July 23, 1965

[. . .] listen, baby, you can get Jeffers in almost any library . . . try his *Such Counsels You Gave to Me,* and his *Roan Stallion, Tamar and Other Poems,* esp. *Roan Stallion.* Jeffers is better on the long poems. I also think that Conrad Aiken, in spite of being a more or less comfortable poetic almost bitch-like type, did manage to plow through some points. His main fault was that he wrote too well; the silk-cotton sounds almost hid the meaning, and, of course, this is the game of most shit-poets: to appear more profound than they are, to sneak in little delicious delicate darts and then retire to their safe comforts. Life gets realer, for me, but it seems most poetry remains the same. I can pick up any issue of *Poetry* Chicago issued in the last ten years and feel like I have been conned and it *is* possible that we *have* been. the trouble with us is that we buy their seeming superiority and therefore they BECOME superior. yet they end up writing for *The New Yorker* and dying and we end up working the coal mines and dying, so does it matter?

The Webbs published two books by Miller after having printed Bukowski's It Catches My Heart in Its Hands *and* Crucifix in a Deathhand.

[To Henry Miller]
August 16, 1965

well, it's my 45th birthday, and on that poor excuse I take the leniency of writing you—although I damn well imagine you get enough letters now to drive you screwy. I even get them, most of them quite lively and even electric. It's when they get down to the poems that they flatten out. and they enclose the poems. listening to Chopin—yeah, Krist, I'm square in some ways, and slugging down the beer. Met your Doc Fink with his jokes about the jews, and also his kind of open plausibility and volume. he brought in the beer along with his wife and I listened and gave him a collage or something I had done. he's your champion but, shit, that's no news—a lot of us are.

anyhow, he gave me a copy of Celine's—what's it called?—*Journey to the End of the Night.* now listen, most writers make me sick. their words don't even touch the paper. thousands of millions of writers and their words, their words don't even touch the paper. but Celine. made me ashamed of the poor writer I am, I felt like tossing it all. a god damned master whispering into my head. god, I was like a little boy again. listening. there's nothing between Celine and Dostoyevsky unless it is Henry Miller. anyhow, after feeling bad after finding out how little I was, I went ahead and read the book, and I was led by the hand, willingly. Celine was a philosopher who knew that philosophy was useless; a fucker who knew that fucking was almost a sham; Celine was an angel and he spit into the eyes of angels and walked down the street. Celine knew everything; I mean he knew as much as there was to know if you only had two arms, two feet, a cock, some years to live or less than that, less than each or any of those. of course, he had a cock. you knew that. he didn't write like [Jean] Genet, who writes very very well, who writes too well, who writes so well that he puts you to sleep. ah hell, and meanwhile, they are shooting from the housetops and the other night they dropped a Molotov at Hollywood Blvd. and Ivar, which is fairly close but not close enough for the kiss of me. I work with niggers and most of them love me, and so maybe I ought to carry a sign around my neck saying, HEY HEY! THE NIGGERS LOVE ME!! but that wouldn't work either because then some white bastard would shoot me. God, woman in here feeding kid and as I write you I lean across and say, "ooooh, try some banana, TRY SOME BANANA!!" me, the tough baby. well, we all come down. they've been in here since the beginning of this letter and I have the radio on and am smoking a cheap cigar along with my beer so if this is garbled it isn't because a green monkey is under the table grabbing my nuts.

drunk, a little, as usual, yes. Chopin winds on under the fingers of . . . who? Pennario, Rubenstein? my ear not that good. Chopin's bones are dead and they are shooting from the housetops and I sit in a dirty noisy kitchen in hell writing to Henry Miller. another beer, another beer. I go on the theory of not quitting; I am not going to quit writing if it all comes back, I am not going to quit if they send in a chorus of whores kicking at my eyeballs and six-boy set of queer drummers bongoing bop havana twist my god. I didn't begin until I was 35 and if I wait 35 more there won't be much left. so, I'm forty-five tonight and writing Henry Miller. that's ok. I think Doc Fink thinks I am a snob. I just don't believe in knocking on doors. I've always been a loner. I'll be straight; I just don't like most people—they tire me, mix me, jiggle my eyeballs, rob me, lie to me, fuck me, fool me, teach me, insult me, love me; but mostly they talk talk TALK until I feel like a cat reamed in the ass by an elephant. it just isn't any good for me, too much of it isn't any good for me. in the factories and slaughterhouses they are kept too busy to talk, and I wish to thank the kindness of my rich bosses for that. even when my bosses fire me I never hear their voices, and I am the most quitting and fired son of a bitch you ever met; but I never hear their voices; it's gentle and delicate and mannerly and I just walk out of the place and don't even think of shooting anybody from a rooftop. I think, well, I'll sleep for a week and then look around. or I'll go home and knock off some ass and drink all night. this kind of thing. I fit in perfectly with those plans. I am a shit. but still a loner. and now I've had a few poems published and they come knocking on the door and still I don't want to see them. the difference being that if you are a loner and nobody, you are a nut; if you are a loner and a little known, then you are a snob. they'll always find the proper shaft to fit you no matter which way you move. even the woman here, she's got to constantly correct me. no matter what the hell I say. I can wake up in the morning and say, "God, it's hot." and she'll say, "You just *think* it's hot. it's not as hot as yesterday. suppose you were in Africa . . ." this sort of thing.

where am I? another beer? of course.

now the little girl wants to work the typer. o.k., work it baby, work it. I pick her up. then down she goes, "God damn it, I tell her, don't you see I am writing Henry Miller? don't you see that it's my 45th birthday?"

anyhow, I hope you got the 3 *Cru[cifi]x*'s. Webb gave me 16 which he shouldn't have because I tend to pass them out to whoever is around while I am drunk plus my paintings, but the paintings are lousy, I think, I keep trying to get the color yellow to show through the other colors, maybe like my backbone. sure, I'm yellow; I'm yellow and I'm tough and I'm tired and I'm drunk, and life parts like a fart and I walk on through. I keep thinking of [D. H.] Lawrence milking his cows, I keep thinking of his Frieda, I am nuts; I keep thinking of faces in factories, in jails, in hospitals. I am not sorry for these faces; I just can't make them out. like berries swaying in the wind, like birdshit on the statue of life. god damn. another beer. well, Franck now on. we take what we can get. although S. in D. not bad. when I was married to this millionairess, I was lying on the rug drunk and listening to F.'s Symphony in D., she sat there and said, "I think that music is *ugly*!" so I knew right then that the million was gone. I couldn't make it with her. and to prove it, that night when I fucked her in the bedroom all the shelves fell down and flowerpots and trinkets came down upon my back and ass. I mean, I do a good job, but not *that* good. she thought it was ugly when I laughed then too, and stuck it back in and saw the million going going . . . "I don't like a man who makes fun of himself, I don't like a man who laughs at himself. I like a man who has pride," she told me. well, I've got to laugh because I am ridiculous; I am only temporarily made, I shit and wipe my ass, am full of snot and slime and bugs and grandiose notions . . . but I really am a turd, nothing but a turd. so, first there was the smooth one with the purple stickpin in his necktie and the cultured voice. but she finally wound up with an Eskimo, a Japanese fisherman and teacher, Tami, I think his name was, is. Tami got the million; I got the stick. I guess they don't listen to Franck.

anyhow, I hope you got the books. the woman went down to the market and got a paper box and chopped it up and did the dirty work. a friend of yours said he'd pay for the books, said, "I'll merely charge it off to office expenses." I suggested that 5 bucks a book would be o.k., and since my royalties are only ten cents a copy on any of 3,000 books sold, I thought I was getting a steal. I guess he thought so too because it's been 2 weeks and I have not heard. but then I did tell him, "If you're short, forget it." and I guess that we are all *short* finally. the grave is always there and we can't buy ourselves out, ever. I lived in a place once in Atlanta for a dollar 25 cents a week. I lived for a month on 8 dollars. and wrote poetry on the edges of dirty newspapers that I found upon the floor. no lights, no heat. I don't know what happened to the newspapers. I kind of remember what happened to me. that's normal, even when it gets abnormal. I give you a lot of wind tonight. are you still reading? I wonder. well, 45 is a sad age. 30 was the worst. I got through that. I do not pretend to have guts. I only wonder.

now get ready for the dirty word: of course, I'd like to meet you. I'd like to see you sitting in a chair across from me. not much chance. I am not much on talk. I don't feel well most of the time. it would be like b.g. meeting God. and then you'd walk across the floor and go to piss, and I'd say, look, God pisses too. don't hate adulation, Henry, you've got some of it coming. you've been through it. I only call you "Henry" because I get these long driveling letters from some student who insists upon calling me "Mr. Bukowski" all the way through until I feel like I've been taken and that really all that he wants to do is crawl across my flattened corpse. anyhow, if you ever decide to arrive, yow, my phone # is NO-1-6385 and the address is on the envelope. but now I am shitting on you. forget it.

Celine, Celine, my god, Celine. that they ever built a man like that??

another beer.

anyhow, since you are Celine, I'd like you to know no matter what the writing, that I've been through it—the park benches, the factories, the jails; guarded door at a whorehouse in Fort Worth, worked in a dog biscuit factory, celled with Public Enemy #1 (what luck!); rolled and been rolled; the hospitals with my belly ripped open; shacking with every whore and mad bitch from Coast to Coast; all the terrible jobs, all the terrible women, everything, and only a little of this comes out in my poetry because I am not yet man enough and perhaps never will be; runoff in late *La Grande Ronde Review* that I was crude, my spelling was weak, and all sorts of blows. I didn't buy the copy, I don't have the guts, but heard from somebody else. they went 5 and one half pages ripping me up. maybe I am getting there?? but what most of them don't realize, tho my spelling is weak, I write a lot of the stuff drunk and the damn fingers skip and the next morning I am too sick to read it, just skip it, get it out, just like I will this letter. the morning is not strong enough to stand the night.

but instead of going on, I think I'll stop; certainly and sure enough I've prob. said enough. after wild beginning have now hit same timeclock for 8 years on horrible job. but other day sold a painting for $20. sight unseen. somebody shot me a twenty from a small town in Florida and said, "ship one of your paintings." so maybe I'm not dead yet. you will never be dead.

[To Henry Miller]
Late August 1965

no, I am not the visiting type, and hope you don't think I am intending to propel myself against you. I was drunk when I wrote the letter, if this is an excuse. as to drinking, if it moils or screws the head off of my creativity, then that is too bad. I need more to live minute by minute than to be any kind of creative artist; what I mean is, I need something to keep me going or I lag, I am a coward, I don't want to walk through doors.

Books [*Crucifix*] paid for, and just in time (for me). had to get complete brake overhaul on my old Plymouth. been driving without brakes. the woman hollers at the price. she thinks I am a fool. I am a fool. she goes in to piss and leaves the door open and I look at her large, lifeless dead legs. then she turns on the radio. the radio is always on. I walk around with ear plugs in my head wondering if I should go out for a bottle of wine. like anybody else—gas bill due, phone bill due, cliffs falling down on my head . . . no, no, I seldom work with prose, mainly because if they turn it down I'm dead. all that energy shot. I don't have the guts to write a novel for fear I'd put half my life into it and then it would lay in a drawer without legs. I once said in a magazine that I'd write a novel for a $500 advance, anywhere, anytime. I didn't get any takers and won't. if I sound money-crazy, don't think I am. it's a matter of energy—seeping out. I can play with poems and hardly get hurt and still keep the fort, if you know what I mean. the kid is clawing at me now—11 months old, she wants to type. she'll get her chance, the bitch.

will try to look up [Jean] Giono or have the woman do it. yet I can't see anybody holding near Celine. this man had a headful of golden screws. shit, shit, my arms and chest ache! I'm going down to Del Mar tomorrow on the train. these women have me hung on a rope in these 2 small rooms, and I must shake free a moment: sky, road, a horse's ass, the dead trees, the sea, new legs of wandering—anything, anything . . . the drawings I sent you terrible. a bad trick. I am doing a book of drawings for somebody and these were 2 I did not send in. this editor wants a lot of drawings and a few poems—which makes it nice: a little india ink and a lot of beer and I'm in.

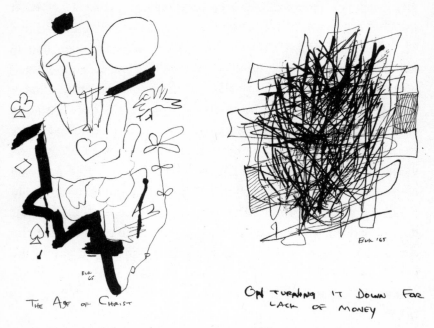

THE AGE OF CHRIST

ON TURNING IT DOWN FOR LACK OF MONEY

Both drawings above, discarded from the unfinished book of drawings and poems *Atomic Scribblings from a Maniac Age* (1966), were sent to Miller.

———

In 1965-66, Bukowski appeared in several issues of Intermission, *edited by Cole.*

[To Gene Cole]
December 1965

Thanks, of course, for *Intermission*. I have read 2 copies so far; good articles, but your filler poetry can use a little shot in the arm. Still it makes me nervous to read those articles on playwriting, "a play must have a premise" and so forth. I am afraid that the problems of our playwrights are the same as everybody else—that is, they are trained, they are TOLD the proper way to do a thing. This may make it go down well, it can help practitioners; it can help bad playwrights become almost good ones, but "how to do it" will never create an Art, it will never shake the old skin, it will never get us out of here. If I were to write a play I'd write it any damn way I pleased and it would come out all right. This is not to say there shouldn't be articles on playwriting or playwriting workshops. I wouldn't outlaw anything. Let the people do as they please. And luck to them. And if they are able to create Art and make a lasting theatre with these methods, I will be most happy to be called a liar.

1966

[To John Bennett]
Late March 1966

[. . .] sometimes when I get drunk, some editor in me sneaks into the veins, into the oblong sagging string of brain and then even I get ideas for mags, to wit:

(and seriously)!

1: *A Contemporary Review of Literature, Art and Music*
   or et:
   A Review of Contemporary Literature, Art and Music.
   no poetry, no original modern work—just articles, lively gutty ones on the scene, and if possible reproductions of Art work. of course, I'd write some of the articles myself to make sure that the mag had life and bang. I do think a magazine of this sort is needed but doubt if it will ever evolve.

2: *The Toilet Paper Review*
   which would be typewritten by me on toilet paper (our motto being, "We Give a Shit!") would use some carbons in typing and then would glue toilet paper to regular paper and make original cover drawing for each mag sent out.

3: (no title) but would hand print in india ink each mag with oil pastel artwork (all different) in each mag, also an original artwork on front of each mag. I learned how to hand-print very fast when I was starving and had no typer and sent the stuff out via inkwave. I can handprint faster than I can write freehand, or I used to be able to. [. . .]

some monkey in Arkansas has ducked out with around 100 india ink drawings of mine which he claimed he was going to bring out in book. advertised book and collected $$$. now he won't respond to my inquiries, my small public is going to think I am a fucking swindler. it's not so much that that I mind, it is the long drunken nights, up all night to sunup, laughing to myself, drinking, balls naked in the kitchen, smearing india ink all

ELEVATOR

Intended for the aborted *Atomic Scribblings from a Maniac Age*, this drawing was eventually published in a literary magazine in 1971.

87

over myself, all over the walls, feeling almost alive about it, you know, and then to have the fucker take all those nights, all those drawings—bury them, tear them. I'd like to nail one of those shits in the doorway when they answer the bell but they must guess damn well I can't run the country chasing them down. easier to do another hundred drawings. so, there's another sad story for your file. the literary type is the last type to trust, remember that. ants, pygmies, hand job artists, cocksuckers, motherboy snot swallowers, the whole lot of them—almost, almost. you've got to remember I'll be 46 in August and even tho I only began in the game at 35, I've seen enough in eleven years to store a napalm kiss for all of them. almost.

Ferlinghetti published the Artaud Anthology *in 1965, which Bukowski reviewed for the* Los Angeles Free Press *in early 1966.*

[To Lawrence Ferlinghetti]
June 19, 1966

[. . .] well, listen, I didn't mean to get off on tangent. on the Artaud, I found many of his thoughts extremely similar to my own, in fact, I had the feeling as I read that I had written many of the lines—bullshit, of course, but he's one of the few writers who makes me feel that I can't write at all. I don't get this feeling very often.

don't worry about the French reviews, those bastards automatically think we're square—it's an insignia they've been wearing for some centuries, it's a witch hunt and a cunt trick. it's the best book, your best, a sledgehammer with legs and eyes.

meanwhile, I palm my battered nuts and shiver in the sun.

Jean and Veryl Rosenbaum published Bukowski's poetry in several Out-cast *issues in 1966–68.*

[To Jon and Lou Webb]
July 11, 1966

yes, Rosenbaum received the *Ole* issue with poem about him. he wrote me. I have the letter here somewhere.

> *Heil Hank! King of the beer cans,*
> *I was really looking to being offended by your reply poem in* Ole *to the literary gauntlet and superb piece of writing by me in* Outcast #1. *I was thus disappointed to hear you only say ouch. It was so feeble maybe it wasn't even an ouch, but a fart. It wasn't your superficial grasp of situations that bored me so but rather that you've lost your punch. as a matter of fact you are just as aware as I that you haven't written an effective poem since* It Catches—, *despite the arranged p.r. on the next two! as two of your real admirers both Veryl and I have worried about your artistic decline these many years, despite your entertaining popularity. I think you are above that scene. Are you aware that your post office insurance policy covers 50 percent of the cost of psychotherapy? I wish you'd do something to uncork yourself, as we need and want some strong things of yours for future issues of* Outcast.
> *Jean*

on pink paper with an *Outcast* head. in the last issue of their *Outcast* they ran off my poem with 3 or maybe only 2 words mis-spelled, not my misspelling but "e's" where "o's" should go and so forth. the other poems were (by other people) not misspelled. no need to hack at infinities, but this is just another time where rubbing up against Jean leaves me with a sense of disgust. and for a man who was not offended, only disappointed in a poem, he comes along in a rather yellow fanged manner in his letter. I don't have to be a psychiatrist to figure he's lashing back. but I'm through haggling with this turkey. by the way, there are a half dozen different post office insurances, that is insurance allowed by the post office to be used by employees. all their rates vary, even including the cost of "psychotherapy." the good doctor just loves to bring up the post office—he knows that it is killing me and it seems to please him. also, I don't get the line "I think you are above that scene." it seems to be thrown into the letter between 2 lines that have no relationship to it. am *I* the *only* one who is nuts? um, um, umm. [. . .]

the thought of a possible 3rd. Bukowski book by Loujon in 67 or early 68 sure does keep me from dropping dead in the streets. just the longshot chance of it happening keeps me tearing down paper walls and going to bed with women I don't want and walking around under that fucking toteboard sun with holes in my soul and pockets. umm. anyhow, it is good to get a sign like this way early. I can be gathering, typing stuff up. have acceptances in 2 dozen lit mags, and in the mail today, letters from couple of European mags that want to see my stuff, and my fingers feel good on paper, on keys. I am not writing the same stuff or the same way as I did in *It Catches*. this bothers some of them, but to me it is only normal. whatever I write, good or bad, must be me, today, what it is, what I am. the drunken room and whore poems were all right in their time. I can't go on and on with that. the Americans always want an IMAGE to catch to, something to label, to cage. I can't give them that. either way they take this old man with holes in his socks, at 4 in the afternoon, rubbing his eyes and dreaming on Andernach, or they take nothing. the last poem on the day I write will be the poem I need to write then. I allow myself this freedom. [. . .]

no, [John] Martin doesn't tend to lecture. I try to get him more on himself and his doings. his printer is a real square. try to get Martin to tell you about the printer sometime. there was a poem of mine with the word "fuck" in it. he set up everything but that word. said he couldn't do it. never had. suggested to Martin that they get a little rubber stamp and stamp it in. my god, the poem never ran. he couldn't do it. he calls my poems "real sadistic." god o mighty, what a world of whammy halfpeople.

[To Harold Norse]
August 2, 1966

[. . .] Creeley, yes, hard to blithe down, but believe he is getting desperate—finally wrote a poem about how he watched some woman pee in the sink, she didn't piss, she pee'd and she blushed, peeing after he had fucked her—only Creeley doesn't fuck he makes love. but the poem didn't work because you knew he was trying to throw a curve and become one of the boys. it's as bad as me trying to be Creeley, say:

I, swung her in the swing
in the park, my daughter, the sky was there,
my daughter in the swing, it was in the
park, and some day, I thought, as she met the sky:
I'll get first
        crack.

[To Michael Forrest]
Late 1966

[. . .] I carve into stone not because it lasts but because it is there and it does not talk back like a wife. I carve into stone because the 2 or 3 good men of a future world will pick me up and laugh. That's enough—my centuries have not furnished me this.

I do think that for (or in spite of) my 46 years in hell that I have retained a splendid little chickenshit glory cockroach spittle of musing + cracked laughter under (perhaps) my left big toenail, which keeps me halfway between suicide and striving.

It is a good middleground. Of course, middlegrounds are neither forceful nor publicly or artistically bombastic (successful) or loveable. Most of my poems are about me simply walking across a room and being glad/sad (no proper words here) that both the room + I are here at the moment. I have read, I think, almost all the books, but still wish somebody somewhere had said this to *me*. N[ietzsche], Shope[nhauer], pretensive crowd-pleasing Santayana. Anybody.

1967

[To Darrell Kerr]
April 29, 1967

[. . .] I mean, for me, a good piece of the action is in the Creation, Kapital Cunt. either fuck it right it write it paint it. 2 guys talking don't do much for me.

writing a poem is a singular thing.

now I am not a snob who thinks my shit doesn't stink but between drinking myself to death and working a job that chews me up, the time left, those one or 2 hours, I like to work with in my own fashion.

so I don't read at poetry readings, go to Love-Ins, Freak-outs, so forth.

I was always basically a "loner." there *are* people like that, either from nature or psychosis or whatever who are in agony in the crowd and feel better alone. YOU MUST LOVE is pretty much the thing now, and I think that when love becomes a command, hatred becomes a pleasure, what I am trying to explain to you is that I have rather cracked grains and that a visit from you would not solve anything, especially with a jug of red eye when my stomach is gone. I am almost 47, drinking for 30 years and there isn't much left, in and out of hospitals. I am not putting on the pity bit. it is only that *some* of the things that some of the young people see now, understand now (and a lot they don't understand), I was onto back in 1939 when War was Good, the Left was Beautiful and so forth. when Hemingway looked pretty good and around there sometime guys were running off to join the Abraham Lincoln Brigade. the young are always excited; I wasn't. the frame in the picture keeps changing and if you run to every pretty-seeming sunrise you are going to get sucked into a lot of sandtraps and dead flags. a man must pretty well form his own conceptions if he can; chittering like an ape in the park or the dark isn't going to do it. In fact, not much is going to do it. I am not going to do it with a typewriter and you are not going to do it with a bookstore. if the world changes at all it will be because the poor are fucking too much and that there are too many fucking poor and the few rich power boys will get scared because if you get enough poor and they are poor enough not all the propaganda newspapers in the world will be able to tell them how lucky they are and that poverty is holy and that starvation is good for the soul. if these people have the vote, things are going to change and if they don't have the vote the riots are going to get bigger redder hotter heller. I have no politics but this is easy enough to see. but the power boys are clever too, they will attempt to give them just a nibble, just enough *alms* to hold them back. then the bomb could solve a lot of things too. all the chosen have to do is wait until there's a hiding place in space and let the thing go. in the right places. they come back after the sanitary men have scrubbed the bones clean. meanwhile I sit at my typewriter, and wait. [. . .]

it is dangerous to move too much out of the poem form. the poem-form (shit, looking out my window now I just saw something get out of a taxi ow ow ow ow in yellow high skirt nylon legs jesus she wobbled in the sunlight and the dirty old man pressed against the window and dropped his tears of blood) keeps it pure for the tooth, silk to the touch, nylon for broken guitar soul, o o yah. but once in a while I slip out of poem-form and shoot mouth. I am only human, "all too human" as some dustly old philosopher once said. dustly, thusly. even the worms fuck. [. . .]

I thought I had won the Pulitzer Prize. Webb told me last year the Pulitzer people had contacted him, that *Crucifix* had been nominated for the Pulitzer. well, either Webb was drunk or somebody else got it. probably gave it to some fat college prof who wrote rhyming rondos in attempt to prove he had psyche. listen, I've got to stop this somewhere. you'd think I was drunk; haven't even had a beer for 2 days. all right. getting dark. Los Angeles is a Cross, and we all hang here, stupid little Christs. 6 p.m. Chinese music on radio. sober, sober, sober.

———————

[To Ronald Silliman]
March 1967

[. . .] I have read the critics—Winters, Eliot, Tate, so forth, the New Criticism, The New New Criticism, the demands of Shapiro, the whole *Kenyon* crowd, the *Sewanee* crowd, I used half a lifetime reading the critics, and while I found the content pretensive I found the style somehow pleasurable, and now it's nice of you to tell me that the best of them are trying to get "human dignity, self-respect, the kind of pride you find in a wild, free stallion" back into verse. that sounds as phoney as a horse's rubber asshole to me but if that is your insight and/or your outlook, it's yours, and fine.

"IF ALL ELSE IS UGLY, IS DEADLY, THEN ISN'T IT OUR *DUTY* TO BE BEAUTIFUL?" you scream at me in large caps. Ronald, "duty" is a dirty word, and "beautiful" is a put down word. you want to knock somebody off his dusty little legs—just demand that he be "beautiful."

[To John Bennett]
September 1967

the little mag world is not too healthy an animal for me. there are 3 or 4 good ones, and after that, nothing. the other day a mag, *Grist,* changed a word in my poem from "chess" to "chase," which with the remainder of the wordage made me seem like a fag. they can have their club, their way, but why force me to join? not feeling well, anyway, I wrote them about it. then there are dozens of other mags who have accepted my poems, only never to come out with an issue, and NEVER returning the work. I don't keep carbons. nor do I believe that my work is that precious, but it is a disgusting thing, the way these high-ideal little mag boys turn out to be pricks, fags, fakirs, fuckups, sadists, so on and so forth. the problem is that most of the boys are very young. a little mag seems like a dramatic thing to them, Art, smashing old barriers, hurrah for bravery, so forth. but to begin with, most of them are bad editors, no money, expect money somehow out of the setup; don't like work, most of them, and are bad writers, most of them; and then just get tired, say fuck it. I've lost a book of poems and drawings to the shits, along with 300 poems. sometimes I think I'd rather deal with the telephone co., the gas co., the police.

[To Robert Head]
October 18, 1967

[. . .] on anti-war poems, I was anti-war a long time ago, at a time when it was not popular or in to be so. it was a very alone situation, World War II. it seems that from the intellectual and artistic viewpoint that there are good wars and bad wars. to me, there are only bad wars. I am still anti-war and anti a hell of a lot of other things, but I still remember the other situation, and how poets and intellectuals change like the seasons, and what trust and stand I have rests mainly within myself, what's left of me, and when I see the long lines of protestors now, I know that their courage is only a kind of semi-popular courage, doing the right thing in proper company, it's so easy now. where the hell were they when *I* was thrown into a cell, World War II? it was very very quiet then. I don't trust the human beast, Head, and I don't like crowds. I drink my beer, hit the typer and wait.

[To Harold Norse]
October 21, 1967

[. . .] p.s.—fucked-up letter, anyhow, on Ginsberg, it's obvious that he has accepted the mantle of the crowd (long ago) and that's bad because once the crowd gives you the mantle and you accept it, they begin to shit on you. but Allen doesn't know this. he thinks he's got enough moxie to overcreep it. not so. his beard stands out and tends to save him but you can't write poetry with a beard. I can barely read his stuff now. his self-proclaimed GOD and LEADER am-I stuff is simply dull and driven. then he's gotta hang on Leary and Bob Dylan, the headline makers. bad moves all. all this is obvious, but nobody says anything about it, mainly because they are a little frightened of Allen as they are a little frightened (more frightened) of Creeley. it's a wasted scene, a little something like a horror movie—you really want to laugh but the air smells bad. I think the whole twisted beastly thing has something to do with the U.S. of America, tho I am not sure. Christ, can Europeans fuck-up like that? I suppose they can, but not with such consistency and accuracy.

———————

[To Harold Norse]
November 3, 1967

[. . .] for it all, *Evergreen* [*Review*] and Penguin, and it's good, we can stand a shot of light just to keep the hacks and jackasses from having a *complete* ball, we've still got to remember where we've come from and what it is. the head must remain where it was. a champ is only as good as his *next* fight; the *last* one won't get him through the first round. writing is a form of staying alive, a food, a gruel, a drink, a hot fuck. this typer cleans and grinds and stabilizes and prays. nobody is ever going to ask me to run for President on a platform of Pot for every Pot. I've had enough bad jobs. and if they want divinity they can seek their corner church. all I need is typewriter ribbons, paper, something to eat and a place to stay—preferably with a window facing the street and a crapper not down the hall and a landlady with good legs who swishes her thighs and behind against you now and then. against me, now and then.

———————

[To Harold Norse]
December 1, 1967

got *Evergreen* 50 today with my short poem in there, way in the back, the thing is shot through with the famous, so there they are: Tennessee Williams, John Rechy, LeRoi Jones, Karl Shapiro, William Eastlake . . . but the writing is all bad, except mine and a really good play by Heathcote Williams, *The Local Stigmatic,* which first played at the Traverse Theatre in Edinburgh . . . whatever that is. anyway, it's good writing. But the Rechy piece was really bad and the Williams and Shapiro almost as bad. but all this I learned a long time ago—the now famous did some good writing at one time and now no longer do good writing but go around attached to their names, their labels and the public and the magazines eat their shit. the gods have blessed me by not making me famous: I still shoot the word out of the cannon—which beats drippings from a limp cock. for it all, though, getting into *Evergreen* did me good because it taught me that everything is nothing and that nothing is everything and that you still have to lace your shoes if you have shoes and make your own magic if there is any to be made. I am more concerned with the longer bullfight poem I did for them and hope it comes out all right in my mind when it comes out. the thing about *Evergreen* is that you might shake somebody alive who you never might have reached before, but this is a tangent. the thing is of course to get the salt and pepper on the meat, get it down, no matter where it appears. there are basic truths, sometimes, I think, and most of the time we forget them. or are dulled out of them or sold out of them. I am probably writing all this shit about *Evergreen* because I have a bad conscience and fear that I am slipping as a good writer in order to get into their slick pages. on the other hand, there is a kind of kid's Christmas joy at opening the big stocking for the goodies. it's nice. after all, after the poem is over, then you are nothing but a chickenshit salesman, and who wouldn't rather appear in *Evergreen* than in *Epos, A Quarterly of Verse*? perhaps the truly good men have not yet arrived. perhaps we are still in the cocoon stage, and worse, will be ripped from our fucking cocoons before our time. ah. umm. I certainly have all the weaknesses of a gang of unschooled seamen just off the boat after 90 days at sea without sleep and very little round-eye. well, I do not pretend to be a Christ-like creature, and anyhow it wouldn't be worth a cat-turd to be a Christ-like creature, don't you think? I don't think.

1968

[To Jack Micheline]
January 2, 1968

[. . .] Yes, you're right—the poem-world is sort of silky and dominated by soft fakes, *Poetry* (Chicago), which, a long time ago, was a good magazine is now the stomping ground and lie-machine for the flabby fake poets, the tricksters, but they watch us—they come around and ring the doorbell, they want to look at the creature and see how it is done. But they see nothing—a red-eyed fart on the couch with a hangover, who talks like the corner newsboy. [. . .]

Fame + immortality are games for other people. If we're not recognized when we walk down the street, that's our luck. So long as the typer works the next time we sit down.

My little girl likes me and that's plenty.

[To Charles Potts]
January 26, 1968

[. . .] I like ACTION. I mean, you know how slow some of the mags move, something very deadening about it—yawn, yawn, oh mother, why do it? you know. I guess a lot of them are waiting for donations or miracles. neither is coming; they might as well face

101

up and shove through. that's one reason I been writing a column a week for *Open City*—so far. ACTION, it jumps from the typewriter onto the page. I hand it to [John] Bryan, ZAP, it EXPLODES, a thing need not be journalism because it is instant, bad and art and good art are created at the same time. I mean time element has nothing to do with it. not explaining this well, trying to make 5 p.m. box.

―――――――――

In 1967, Bukowski unsuccessfully applied for a National Endowment for the Arts fellowship.

[To Harold Norse]
April 20, 1968

[. . .] wrote Carolyn Kizer for another application blank to wearily try again for a grant. I'd heard about some of those who were given grants and knew that they were not very much—I mean, so far as talent. also some were offered grants who didn't even apply, and some of these refused the grants. I guess they are not as near to starvation and madness as I am. near that end. well, nothing from dear Carolyn, but I suppose it takes time. but I heard so quickly the other time. and a nice long letter, what happened? one wonders about things that occur underground and overground that we know nothing of. I guess the X is chalked on my back. I'm ready for the butcher. the F.B.I. was around the other day, asking my landlord and the neighbors about me. the landlord told me. since I drink with the landlord and his wife, I've got the pipe-line. [Douglas] Blazek told me about a year or 2 ago the F.B.I. came around to him and asked about me. you know, the National Foundation is govt. sponsored? *that* could be Carolyn's silence and maybe I've fucked you too. think I told you a bigwig interviewed me in a long dark room with a lamp down at the end of big table. real Kafka-nazi stuff. I was told they didn't like my column "Notes of a Dirty Old Man." I asked, "are we to presume that the postal officials are the new critics of literature?" "uh, no, we didn't mean that." like hell. then he told me, "if you had stuck to poetry and poetry books you would have been all right." "but this . . ." and he tapped the newspaper and my column, and left the rest unspoken. it is the writing itself that simply pisses them, but I'm hardly even obscene. they don't know how to hook me. and we keep shaking hands. but they are waiting for my one slip and then they are going to step in and break my neck. meanwhile, they are hoping that I will get paranoid about the whole thing and start jumping at shadows and flush my supplies of luck down the crapper. which I damn well might do. meanwhile, I tell the few people I know so they can get off me if they wish. and it's amazing. have told a few and no longer hear from them. most everybody, I've found out, is some kind of shit, deep down. I am the siffed-up redhead being let out of the car on the corner.

———————

[To d. a. levy]
July 16, 1968

[. . .] rec. *The Buddhist [Third Class Junkmail] Oracle* bundle today. mah thanks, surely. paper has a curious flavor of its own. I am sure that you have discovered what I have discovered—that the poetry game is all right the way we have been working it, but so many clogs, over half the poems accepted never published and simply forgotten by little yawning people in Peoria Heights . . . meanwhile, these papers give INSTANT ACTION that you can SEE FEEL . . . SWING INTO AGAIN AND AGAIN . . . who the hell wants to rot and wait??? we work with all hands . . . everything counts.

1969

Dombrowski published Charles Bukowski. A Critical and Bibliographical Study, *by Hugh Fox, in 1969. It was the first lengthy critical study of Bukowski's work.*

[To Gerard Dombrowski]
January 3, 1969

[. . .] On the Fox book on me—all right, I drank a few nights with the man, and if you want some stinking gossip—he is not my type. He is University and caught between the squeezed balls of his teachings. Perhaps my resentment is that on the nights of our drinking, he did all the talking, and a lot of it was lousy spoiled soft blasé butterball extension of guarded resentments and mistreatments of an Ivy League English II spieler . . . he got liad laid, he didn't get laid . . . I wondered what some of the guys living in 5 bucks a week rooms or on park benches or at The Mission would have thought . . .

You know, the main problem, so far, has been that there has been quite a difference between literature and life, and that those who have been writing literature have not been writing life, and those living life have been excluded from literature. There have been breakthroughs through the centuries, of course—Dos[toyevsky], Celine, early Hem[ingway], early Camus, the short stories of Turgenev, and there was Knut Hamsun—*Hunger,* all of it—Kafka, and the prowling pre-revolutionary Gorky . . . a few others . . . but most of it has been a terrible bag of shit, but since 1955 there has been a throwback of the bag of shit. Of course, there have been a terrible lot of turds ghostly thrown upon us and swallowed (publicly) since then, but now we are in a state of mould and there hasn't been much breakthrough because all the good writers write pretty god damned well but by god very much alike, and so now we are in another flux???? . . . no GIANTS.

Well, maybe we don't need GIANTS. Somehow, the giants have seemed to have left us fairly well short-changed. what? But then, too, I grow damned tired of the competent and even *human* writer. The answer is somewhere in the salami sky, and I mean of the spirit, not those idiots bumbling the moon. The first atrocity on the moon, the first war won't be long in coming. Perhaps the first atrocity was the human foot upon the untouched.

Well, you asked me about the Fox book on me. You want it straight? It was dull, straight, academic and uncourageous. It was textbook frogs hopping their dull lily pad hops. Dull; I said it twice; I'll say it thrice: dull, dull, dull. THE POEM-MESSAGE or FORCE was completely overlooked in the mama-taught thing of this belongs here and that belongs there—: this is this school, and that is that school. Fuck that. I used to g.d. have to fight the bullies all the way home from grammar school to college, and they used to follow me, mocking me, daring me, but there was always more than one, and I was one, and they knew I had something packed in me somewhere. They hated it; still do.

Bergé submitted her poetry to Laugh Literary and Man the Humping Guns, *coedited by Bukowski and Neeli Cherkovksi in 1969–71.*

[To Carol Bergé]
February 25, 1969

Ah, shit, Carol, these are not very good. I am sitting here drunk + it is raining, has been for days, and these are not very good.

"Edges" closest–certain bad lines:

"Soft hand shake"

"Weak cop-outs"

"Avenging knife"

What the fuck, Carol? What the fuck you giving me?

And no return envelope?

"Edges" still the best of these.

But your last line terrible. 19th century French-literary Romanticism. What the fuck. You know this.

I am going to put out a good magazine. And doing so sometimes means being cruel and being cruel sometimes means being right.

———————

Thomas befriended Bukowski after accepting two of his poems for Notes from Underground *2, which he guest-edited in 1966.*

[To Harold Norse]
February 26, 1969

[. . .] Honorable Honorable John Thomas, the well-bred and well-read, all too-well read, tells me very solemnly afterwards, "you get dull when you're drunk, Bukowski." he always *has* to call me Bukowski as if we were before an audience and it was nec. that we be identified. J.T. has a headful of words and ideas, very well organized, but placid, a placid art, strong and organized, but placid, a horse-ass machinegun mounted on a shiny tripod and shooting its precious bullets. as per Pound, Olson, Creeley, the same dry sand, yet I have listened to the man because he can be humorous in a vicious sort of way. in my cups, when I tell him that Life is truly horrible, the people, the structure, the death-ending, the whole mess, and he'll say, "you never signed any *contract*, Bukowski, saying that Life must be beautiful." and then he leans back and licks his lips a little, he makes his living with his tongue and his lips and his cock, a most beautiful woman supports him while he lounges around in his big beard and big ass and blue jeans. this is to be admired, and, in a minor sense, despised. I've told him that I consider you the greatest living poet and then he just rather snorts (I think he really wants me to tell him that he is) and gets up and reads me some really terrible stuff by Creeley or Olson, and I just sit and listen and don't remark, but the writing itself is so flat and mathematic and automatic and strained that old Blackbeard just finally sighs, himself, goes sits in his chair and stares at me. it's nice to know a Thomas and let him shoot all his guns at you. I think slowly and will listen to his stuff and then finally I will say, "just one moment." and then *I* will say something. in rejoinder, not out of defense but out of simple weariness. and he'll say: "oh, Ojenius Ormegus said that 200 b.c. before his disciples on the tentgrounds of outer Athenia before the Cyclopean War." but at least Thomas has some scratch. the English professors just come around here and lick my balls, and they are all alike, tall, soft, gangly shits, trying to write TOUGH STUFF ABOUT LIFE. god. 3 months off a year to write terrible novels, to awaken me out of bed and show me their poetry—tough guy stuff—and share a 6 pack and stare at me and wonder why I am so fat and tired and thin and worn and sick and angry and dull and uninterested. or, you have the other types, the snob rich types with a home on the coast in Calif. and one in Louisiana and say "homes make a man poor, drain his resourses," and then write modern novels taken from your letters and will not return your letters when you ask for them because they will help keep you alive. you only pay rent. you're lucky. so long as you've got the rent, what do these pricks TELL their students in ENGLISH CLASS I or II? it must be holy sickening . . . these Ph.D. boys who never missed a meal or fell to the floor drunk or turned on the gas, without fame or flame for 3 hours . . . what do they tell those kids???? what CAN they tell them? nothing. so, therefore, everybody appears to be COOL KOOL AND INTELLIGENT and this is the façade and the fish-smell of the wasted centuries. [. . .]

I never get tired of telling you how well you write and you must get used to this. I detest all all almost all writing. *si,* it now is so very good to tell somebody how well they can do it. The Russian Dos had it. Turgenev more than Chekhov. although both were too much of shitted on stylism. Hem had a style that fit but could only pour blood into it through the first half of his work. you are the only honed and smitten realist of the pure Norse-style. I know why W. C. Williams bit on you. you got the muzzle off the mouth that was on *him.* he had 3 or 4 goodies. you are simply consistently splendid and immortal. whenever I read you my own writing gets better—you teach me how to run through glaciers and dump stiffed-up whores. this is not saying it well, but you know what I mean. god damn you, Norse, I've just burnt a tray full of French fries while WRITING about you! and I haven't eaten all day, noel, eeyee, now it is TWO days, and some drunk is beating on an upturned garbage can outside and soon we will all be in jail, soon we will all be . . . little sliced pickled beets labeled in a can . . . oh god, what shit, oh god, what a trap . . . but I didn't sign a CONTRACT, did I? and what's a "contract"—

: their language

––––––––––––

Picasso did not print Bukowski's poems in her literary magazine.

[To Paloma Picasso]
Late 1969

thank you for the personal letter. I was going to send stuff anyhow but just didn't want to jam some piss on you. [Sinclair] Beiles had told me about your project, and I consider his 3 poems which I printed in my own little rag *Laugh Literary* to be the best in manner of writing, in form, in humour, life and flow that I have seen in some years. so you know about Sinclair, but I have my own troubles. I am one of the few who think that Burroughs is not some kind of walking god. I think his cutups and tape arrangements are just ghetto bored flip of a safe and secure man. the adding machine co. has added him up with $$$. it's so easy, but don't let me act like a bitch. I'm far from it. it is only that I say what I say and always have. I let my ringworm mind roll free. I decided long ago in New Orleans alleys while living on nickel candy bars to always let my mind roll free. this does not mean being a "nut." or maybe it does. anyway, while I am pounding here at 2 a.m. in the morning while sitting in between 2 torn desk lamps upon a typewriter table given to me by dead parents as a birthday gift and typing upon a typer given to me for nuttin', while listening to bad piano music upon a 19 dollar Thrifty drugstore radio, I talk, having walked off the job again tonight, to come here and try to take out the 3 or 4 bad lines in the poems enclosed and having by now drunk eleven (bottles of beer) haha—where was I?

oh.

so I have written these new poems in the last 2 weeks, and it could be that a man simply can't write too many good poems in 2 weeks. I don't believe it. I believe that whatever is necessary is necessary, it is up to you. unfortunately or fortunately I feel my power more and more each passing day, each passing year, of course, there are minor lulls wherein I sincerely think of murdering myself and come very close, especially with hangover. however, this is probably common with most of us.—oh, it was BRAHMS!—damn, I didn't know he wrote such lousy piano stuff. . . . o, other things you know—down on Ezra P., just can't read the *Cantos;* they hurt my head, don't go down well. what's wrong with me? could it be simply some shit-mad ego? yet, there seems a balance. for instance, down at work, in the cage, I am a big guy—235 pounds, easy, don't argue, nearing 50, I know I have pissed most of myself away—they don't know I write on the side—that gang really works me over—I only laugh—they don't grasp it—one guy even accused me of being a cocksucker—I only laughed—I have to laugh at their anger—it is beautiful and vicious and forceful—a work of Art—I enjoy them and yet they sicken me—mostly because of the same damned trend—they can't get off the hate-knock trend and it wears . . . wears.

well, I have found that covering letters to submissions almost always mean a bad submission. well. anyhow, this court drunk. I live in the last skid row court in Hollywood. they are drunk here night and day. lesbians trying to be women. women trying to be lesbians. all that. I have a 28 year old girl banging on my door and writing me a 7 page letter every day. she used to dance with an 8 foot cobra. or was it a boa-constrictor? I am really not as mad as I seem, and enjoy quietness, drunkenness, the horseraces and looking upon women's legs sheathed in tight nylon, kicking their slim ankles and looking into what is left of their soul and my soul with their own eyes . . .

of course, shit, hope you can find a poem or two in these; if not return those you cannot use, or the works. rejection is good for the soul. my soul is now a mule.

1970

The introduction below was originally published in Dronken Mirakels & Andere Offers, *translated by Belart into Dutch, but it has never been printed in English.*

[To Gerard Belart]
January 11, 1970

[. . .] "Introduction"

Looking over these poems—to put it simply and perhaps melodramatically: they were written with my blood. They were written out of fear and bravado and madness and not knowing what else to do. They were written as the walls stood, holding out the enemy. They were written as the walls fell and they came through and got hold of me and let me know of the sacred atrocity of my breathing. There is no out; there is no way of winning my particular war. Each step I take is a step through hell. I think the days are bad and then the night comes. The night comes and the lovely ladies sleep with other men—men with faces like rats, with faces like toads. I stare up at the ceiling and listen to the rain or the sound of nothing and I wait for my death. These poems came out of that. Something like that. I will not be entirely alone if one person in the world understands them. The pages are yours.

[To Marvin Malone]
April 4, 1970

[. . .] my hope is that the *Wormwood Review* goes on as long as you do. I have watched the magazines since around the late 30's, so I can't cover for *Blast* or the early *Poetry, A Magazine of Verse*. But I would place *Wormwood* on top along with the old *Story* magazine, *The Outsider, Accent, Decade,* a very definite force in the moulding of a lively and meaningful literature. if this sounds stuffy, let it. you've done a blockbuster job.

let me roll a smoke. there. yes, I understand your wish not to hear from the prima d's, but I'd like you to know I'm not a p.d. you might have heard some shit and scam on me but I'd advise you to ignore gossip. I *am* a loner, always have been, and just because I've had a few madrigals published doesn't mean I'm going to change my ways. I never did like the literary type, then or now. I drink with my landlady and landlord; I drink with x-cons, madmen, fascists, anarchists, thieves, but keep the literary away from me. christ, how they bitch and carry on and gossip and cry and suck. there are exceptions. Richmond is one. there's no bullshit about him. I can drink 5 or ten cans of beer with Steve and he will never come up with the sad literary bullshit, or any kind of bullshit. you ought to hear him laugh. but there are other types. many other types. mothers' boys. salesmen. pitchmen. weaklings. sucks. vicious little fawns. [. . .]

yes, I'm hustling via the typer and brush, what the fuck. and it has been a fine life—and I've made it writing and painting exactly the way I've felt like it. how long I can stay on top of the water, I don't know. your offer of $10 for 2 poems, damn gracious. well, since I'm hustling, can we cut that in half? how about $5 for 2 poems? can you make that? that would make $20 on the 8 poems, when published. the reason I hustle is not only the kid—for that's a sob story, after all, even if I do love her—but it's hard to typewrite down on skid row, you know. so, Malone, if you can make the 20 I'll take the 20, whenever, all right?

———

[To John Martin]
May 10, 1970

[. . .] I can't agree with you on the dictionary idea for the novel [*Post Office*], but if you insist, we'll go ahead, keep writing down words. I think though that most of the terms are obvious, even to an outsider. but I'm glad enough that you are probably going to do the novel, so I'll compromise if nec. I do think the dictionary has a cheapening and commercial effect, however. Think it over a while.

———

[To John Martin]
[?July] 1970

[. . .] On *Post Office,* I have located the "perfect English" spot that (which?) bothered me. If you want to let it run that way, all right. But I hit my toe on it right away and it may have even been in the original manu. Page 5:

3rd line: "and did not get paid." It seems a little precious. "and didn't get paid" seems less precious. however, either way. every time I look at the novel it looks better. I think I got away with what I intended—that is not to preach but to record. yeah, it'd be nice if we got movie rights and we both got rich, how do we split 50/50? your contract. I can see you in a big office with full-paid staff. and me in an old shack in the hills living with 3 young girls at the same time. ah, the dream!

[To Carl Weissner]
July 11, 1970

[. . .] on *Post Office* I get a lot of delay action from John Martin, who is a good guy but who is doing too many things at once. he claims that I wrote *Post Office* while I was a little bit out of my head—that transition period after quitting the eleven year hitch. well, it's true I was balled-up. he says it's a good novel . . . maybe even a great one but that I got my tenses balled-up and have participles dangling, all that. he says he has to straighten out the grammar and then get some typescripts made. I don't agree with that. I think it should read exactly as written. John has done a lot of good things for me but there's a lot of square in him. he won't admit it but all the writers he prints, except one, are not very dangerous or new; they are quite safe, but Martin makes money, so balls . . . that proves a point of some sort. he even wanted me to write a little dictionary-like thing in front explaining some postal terms. I wasn't for this and tried to get him off that, but he wrote back and explained that I was just feeling bad because I had lost at the track. the man treats me much like an idiot of some sort. I was going on a radio program one night and he phoned me and tried to tell me what to SAY. "listen, John," I had to tell him, "which one of us is Bukowski?" but writers have to put up with this editor thing; it is ageless and eternal and wrong.

John says he wants to hold back on *Post Office* until *The Days*

[*Run Away Like Wild Horses Over the Hills*] has sold out. he says that when a new book comes out the old ones stop selling, so now we must wait. "I assure you," he writes, "that the Germans would not accept *Post Office* in its present form." what the hell is this? nobody corrected the grammar in *Notes* [*of a Dirty Old Man*]. I have signed a contract with him and he has an option on my next 3 books, so there's that. and I don't think he wants to turn loose of the typescripts until he's ready to do the book himself in English. of course, if I'm still around and you and Meltzer are still around I'll ship you and a couple of others over there a typescript and then we can hope for acceptance by somebody and some haggling? christ. and I'll have to go over his grammar-corrected version and put some of myself back into it. he says the book will be out in the Fall or the Winter or something, but somehow I sense a drag-on. the books he has published have been pretty safe so far and in *Post Office* there is a lot of fucking and railing around and perhaps some madness. I think it is better than *Notes* and I wrote short machine-gun style chapters in hope of giving verve and pace and getting away from the novel atmosphere which I hate.

Don't get me wrong, John is a fine person but I feel here that he is a little afraid of publishing the book. it is far more raw than literary and I think subconsciously he is afraid that it will spoil his rep. so there we have all this—a dead stale thing and I feel locked in. [. . .]

By the way, I have sold 3 or 4 chapters from the novel to the dirty mags, one of them out the other day; already paid for the others. that's before I mailed the typescript to Martin, which is like sending one of your children to the fucking tombs. anyhow, I typed the stories right out of the typescript and I didn't hear any complaints about dangling participles. I really ought to mail this letter to Martin instead of to you, but he'd only come on with the father advice. I even told him once, "Christ, you act like my father." Then I told him, "Maybe I ought to name you co-author of *Post Office*."

"O, no, no, you don't understand. I'm not changing your style or anything. I want you to come through just as you are. But I assure you that the Germans would never . . ."

"Yes, father."

"Look, I've been phoning you, Bukowski, but you're never in. Have you been on a toot or playing the horses?"

"Both."

So there it is, Carl, a rather greasy sticky mess. I have some scenes where flowerpots fall on the guy's ass while fucking, taken from my life. my wife. a dirty place on a hill with flies and an idiot dog. part of the book. my wife vomiting while chewing the assholes of Chinese snails, myself hollering, "Everybody's got assholes! Even trees have assholes, only you can't see them!" so on and so on.

guy phoned me. "I read that bit in the dirty mag. is that from your novel?"

"yeh."

"Christ, it's rich! When's the novel coming out?"

"There are some technical holdups."

"Tell him to get it out. I can't wait."

"I'm afraid," I tell him, "you'll have to." [*"told"* –ha ha ha! added in handwriting] [. . .]

all right, I guess I bitch too much tonight. I'm just some guy from Andernach. which somebody told me is a crappy square city. well, blame Andernach on me too. Andernach is a dangling participle, a dry pussy, a fly in the icewater . . . But I was born there and when somebody says, "Andernach" I grin and say, "yeh." let them hang me for that. and that's about that.

[To Robert Head and Darlene Fife]
August 19, 1970

It appears to me that some members of The Women's Lib. are attempting to impose a censorship upon freedom of expression, a censorship which exceeds even the ambitions of some city, county, state and govt. groups out to practice the same ends and methods. A man can write a story about fucking or even lousy women without being a woman-hater. The sisters must realize that limitations on certain forms of writing will eventually lead to control and limitation of all forms of writing except that chosen by some sanctioned body. A writer must be allowed to touch upon everything. Celine was accused of being anti-semitic and when asked about a certain passage—"The Jew's heavy footsteps . . . ," he stated, "I just don't like *people*. In this case it happened to be a Jew." Certain groups are more sensitive to being mentioned than others. Certain people object to being used as models. After Thomas Wolfe's first novel, he couldn't go home again. Until later. Until he had been justified and sanctioned by the critics. Until he had made money. Then his people were proud to be in his novels. Creation can't bear up under restrictions. Tell the sisters to keep their panties kool. we all need each other.

[To Harold Norse]
September 15, 1970

there's nothing to write. I'm hung up by the balls. the stories come back as fast as I can write them. it's over. of course, I land with poems. but you can't pay rent with poems. I'm very down, that's all. there's nothing to write. no hope. no chance. finis. Neeli writes that he sees *Notes of a Dirty Old Man* and Penguin 13 everywhere. now *Notes* has been translated into the German, got a good review in *Der Spiegel*—German *Newsweek*—circulation one million, but for all that, my stuff might as well have been written by Jack the Ripper. very difficult to go on. first check in 2 months today—a lousy $50. story for a dirty magazine about a guy in a nuthouse who climbs the wall, gets on a bus, pulls a woman's tit, jumps off, goes into drugstore, grabs a pack of smokes, lights up, tells everybody he's God, then reaches over, lifts a little girl's dress and pinches her butt. guess that's my future. finis finis finis. Hal, I'm down. can't write.

[To Lafayette Young]
October 25, 1970

[. . .] I have to drink and gamble to get away from this typewriter. Not that I don't love this old machine when it's working right. But knowing when to go to it and knowing when to stay away from it, that's the trick. I really don't want to be a *professional* writer, I wanna write what I wanna write. else, it's all been wasted. I don't want to sound holy about it; it's not holy—it's more like Popeye the Sailor Man. But Popeye knew when to move. So did Hemingway, until he started talking about "discipline"; Pound also talked about doing one's "work." that's shit, but I've been luckier than both of them because I've worked the factories and slaughterhouses and park benches and I know that WORK and DISCIPLINE are dirty words. I know what they meant, but for me, it has to be a different game. it's just like a good woman: if you fuck her 3 times a day, 7 days a week, it usually isn't going to be much good. everything has to be set. of course, I remember one, it worked that way with her. of course, we were drinking wine and starving and had nothing else to do except worry about death and rent and the steel world, so it worked with us. (Jane.) but now I'm so old and ugly and the girls seldom come around anymore, so it's horses and beer. and waiting. waiting on death. waiting on the typewriter. it's easy to be smartass and brilliant when you're 20. I wasn't because I was always rather subnormal in my way. now I'm stronger and weaker, but now with the blade against my throat, my choice OR not, it's there, very much. and I haven't loved life very much; mostly it's been a very dirty game. born set up to die. we're nothing but bowling pins, my friend. [. . .]

Guy Williams tried to pump the English dept. for funds for a reading. Auden getting $2,000. others usually get 3 to 500. poor Williams. he musta caught a wagonload of shit. the English dept. didn't want Bukowski. o.k., maybe they're right. I got two "d's" in English at L.A. City College. anyhow, Williams got $100 from the Art dept. funds to put me on a poetry reading! I hope it doesn't jam him up. believe I've told you that readings are the purest of sweating hells for me, but I slipped myself out on the hustle trip when I laid down those god damned letters in the post office and nobody's going to pay the rent for me because I'd rather lay around all day, drink beer and listen to Shostakovich, Handel, Mahler and Stravinsky. so, I read. my last reading, Cal State Long Beach, I vomited first, then read with drops of sweat dripping down on the table, which I wiped away with my fingertips. but there's another part of me that sees it through. Well, if Auden's worth 2 grand, maybe he'll teach us something. probably how to be fucked.

The short story Bukowski discusses below is "Christ with Barbecue Sauce," published in a tabloid newspaper in 1970.

[To William and Ruth Wantling]
October 30, 1970

[. . .] I sent you the story because I thought you both might *see*. that cannibals can be human too, just as spiders are spiders. I mean, what you need you need, it's implanted there. morals are merely the democratic or fascistic cling-together of minds that see the same picture, formula, code or whatever. it's all basic; there's no argument. good guys don't suck their own dicks. do they?

the story was taken from a news dispatch which I didn't see but which somebody told me about while I was drinking with him and his wife. he's a prof now and I told him it wasn't worth it, that they'd cut off his balls, not right away but eventually. of course, his wife likes it and I like his wife, which confuses everything. lots of profs I don't even let in the door; I tell them I have the flu and I usually have, grab their god damn beer, say thanks, sit in the dark and hope for Mozart or Bach or Mahler, sp. Mahler, and drink the shit. where was I? o yeah, the news dispatch. I took the story from there. the way it went, I think, they picked these people up in Texas and as they pulled them over to the side, one of them was just nibbling the last of the meat from the fingerbones. well, I was drinking when I heard this and I thought it was very funny. I mean, yes. you know, babes, I've worked in a slaughterhouse twice, and when you see enough bleeding meat everywhere you know that just meat is meat and that meat somehow got trapped, that's all. now I'm not begging to get caught and roasted and eaten. I'm old but I carry a good piece of steel in my left pocket and unless they catch me drunk or trusting (see Caesar) somebody is going to see a bit of their own blood. where were we? anyhow, I thought it was a very funny story. Cannibals in Texas. I think a lot of M.D.s, surgeons, esp. are cannibals but don't have the balls to swing all the way over, so they just fuck and snip around. the story, the story. I'm drinking. moiled. lla lllaa, la la, all I tried to do was to tell what made it happen that way and to show that, basically, it was not a CRIME but a FUNCTION caused by SOMETHING.

it's a humorous story because it admits to all human possibilities without guilt; the humour of it being that we are only taught the dignified conceptions and possibilities of a dreary mathematic called Life.

[To John Martin]
[?November] 1970

Enclosed some hack work. I don't claim it to be anything else. Now that I've got these 4 columns up for *Candid Press,* let's see what they do. I don't mind making a little change writing off the elbow. I feel that I am too old to be destroyed—creatively—it's ingrained like death, no shaking it off. But, basically, writing is a very hard hustle and I do like to see some $$$$ coming in. Good for the spirit.

Don't get me wrong. When I say that basically writing is a hard hustle, I don't mean that it is a bad life, if one can get away with it. It's the miracle of miracles to make a living by the typer. And your help has been a hell of a morale boost. You'll never know how much. But writing takes discipline like everything else. The hours go by very fast, and even when I'm not writing, I'm jelling, and that's why I don't like people around bringing me beer and chatting. They cross my sights, get me out of flow. Of course, I can't sit in front of the typer night and day, so the racetrack is a good place to let the juices FLOW BACK IN. I can understand why Hemingway needed his bull ring—it was a quick action trip to reset his sights. With the horses, it is the same with me. I have all these people in the bull ring and I must perform the movements. That is why when I lose I take it so hard. First, I can't afford it; second, I realize that I have made the wrong movements. The horses can be beat if a man makes an art of it, but at the same time, horses eat your leisure time, and that's what a writer needs. So, I try to play everything accordingly—the leisure time when it is proper and the juices flow and the typer hums. when the typer is still, it is back to the bull ring. to test my accuracy on the movements. I guess that I am not very clear here. ah, well.

[To Curt Johnson]
December 3, 1970

The byline leave-off o.k.

Just glad I could curve one by you guys. That $45 check didn't bounce anyhow and allowed me to get some repairs on my old '62 Comet to get it running again so I could get around to my chickenshit poetry readings where I read half-drunk and hustle up a few more bucks. Now listening to Haydn. I gotta be crazy. Enjoyed writing the story, though. Read in the paper where they had caught some cannibals somewhere—Texas I think—and when they pulled them over this gal was just cleaning the meat off the fingers of a hand, nibbling . . . I took it from there.

[To Gerard Belart]
December 4, 1970

[. . .] Somebody just gave me a copy of *Castle to Castle* the other night, so don't send, but thanks. I'm reading it now. Not up to *Journey* . . . He's got a good bitch going in the book but he's standing too *close* to himself. It does lack the humour through horror of *Journey* . . . the truth always makes one laugh especially if it's a truth put in a certain way and a certain style. But I guess he just got his ass kicked once too often; a man finally bends and breaks and loses that little touch . . . great Art is pure ranting in a golden cage. Here Celine just rather throws spoiled apples at us and bits of snot. Still, on the other hand, if *Castle* had been written by anybody *but* Celine, I would have said, "Say here, look, this isn't bad at all!" But it's like with Beiles—you compare only the best to the best. You can't help it. Once a man has leaped 18 feet straight up into the air and then comes back and only leaps 13 feet, it's just not enough for us.

[To Norman Moser]
December 15, 1970

Well, we've all come through our bits or we're dead. Or we're living and dead—"this man's dead life / that man's life dying /" Spender the Steven when he was going good . . . Now, hell, I've lost that thing you sent me, asked me to write something about something, so I've got to coast through in the form of a personal letter. Do with it what you like. We've come a long way, or have we?—since I laid that ten or twenty on you when you had the sleeping bag and your sheaf of poems, and I said that this poem was all right and that I didn't care for that one, and the guy picked out one of your worst and said, "Now, this is a *poem* . . ." I didn't understand that at all, and I guess we were drinking, and it all came down around that poem, you and the guy railing, and then he booted you out, and I remember your tears . . . your wrapping notebooks and dirty stockings all up with rope. It was sad, hell yes, it was sad. and we went down the stairway together and you said, "Bukowski, I don't have any place to stay." And I said, "Look, kid, I'm a loner. I can't stand people, good people or bad people; I've got to be alone . . . Christ, get yourself a room . . ." and I slipped you a bill and ran away into the night. Bukowski, the great understander was a coward. Bought you off, I did. Just to be alone with my own bones. You looked more comfortable the last time I saw you, after my poetry reading at U[niversity of] N[ew] M[exico], even though I was a bit drunk you looked, I noticed, comfortable and calm enough, and you mentioned the old days, the bill I had slipped into your hand, and so it was a bit strange and funny there, so many miles and years from where it had first happened, both of us older, especially me, and both of us still alive. well.

So getting back to the sheaf mailed me and some questions asked or pondered or whatever . . . of course, these are monumental times . . . all our times have been monumental because each man's life is, 1970, 1370, 1170 . . . Of course, there's little doubt that the pitch has been stepped-up. There is the possibility that for the first time in history we are not in a war of nation against nation but color against color—White, Black, Brown, Yellow. There's a fierceness in the streets, a hatred. The trouble with the White race is that too many of them hate each other; this is true in other races but not to our degree. We lack the cohesion of Brotherhood. The only thing we have is a certain terrible brain power and cleverness and the ability to fight at the proper time, the ability to out-trick, out-think, and even out-gut the opposition. No matter how much the White man may hate himself, he is simply *gifted,* but it may be ending for one reason or another. . . . Spengler's *The Decline of the West,* written so many years ago . . . the signs are showing . . . Either Whitey's finally got to get some SOUL or all his cleverness will be just so much spilled jism . . .

Perhaps this wasn't what your sheaf was speaking of anyhow. I've had too many drunken nights and depressive days since I received it. And I always lose everything— jobs, women, ballpoint pens, fistfights, requests for grants from The National Foundation of the Arts, so forth . . . where was I?

Oh yes, I must say, anyhow, that it is dangerous for a poet to pose as prophet, a poet/writer to pose as prophet. Here in the U.S. most serious writers write for many years before they are heard from or recognized, if ever. Unfortunately, many damn fools are recognized because their minds are close to the public mind. Generally a writer of force is anywhere from 20 years to 200 years ahead of his generation, so therefore he starves, suicides, goes mad, and is only recognized if portions of his work are somehow found later, much later, in a shoebox or under the mattress of a whorehouse bed, you know.

All right, then. Let's say a great U.S. writer finally makes it . . . meaning that he will finally not have to worry about paying the rent and will even go to bed with a pretty fair-looking hunk of woman now and then. Most of them have endured (the writer not the woman) anywhere from 5 to 25 years of non-recognition— and when they finally *get* their bit of recognition, they can't control it. Ape? Hell, yes! This t.v. station? o.k? whatcha want me to talk about? yeah, I'll talk. Whatta ya wanna know about? World history? The meaning of Man? Ecology? The Population Explosion?

The Revolution? Whatcha wanna know? *Life* mag photographer? Sure, let him in!

Here's a guy who'd been drinking cheap wine in a small room for 15 years, had to walk down the hall to the bathroom to take a crap. And when he typed, old ladies beat on their ceilings and floors with broom handles, scaring hell out of him . . .

"Shut it up, you fool!"

Suddenly out of some trick, he's known . . . His work is banned, or he walked down Broadway with his pecker hanging out during the Santa Claus Parade and they found out he was a poet . . . Anything will do. Talent helps but it is not always necessary. One of the greatest sentences was said, not by a philosopher but by a baseball player who always had trouble keeping his average near .250 . . . Leo Durocher: "I'd rather be lucky than good . . ." This was because Durocher knew that ten or twelve lucky-bounce singles through the infield meant the difference between the minors and the majors.

So you've got the good old U.S.A. At this moment there are probably only a dozen writers who can write with verve and the grand fire. Of these, let's say, two have been recognized (somehow, luck), 8 will go to their graves without ever being published anywhere. The other 2 will be found and dug-up later by some accident of chance.

So what happens when one of the dozen greats finally lucks it into the limelight? Easy. They kill him. He has lived in those small rooms and starved for so long that he believes he deserves everything that is coming to him—so he sells out, trying to fill in the blanks of the lonely years . . .

> *"Dear Mr. Evans:*
> *Will you write us something about the Black-White*
> *Question or Hippies or Where Are We Going in America*

*Today? Something on that order. You may be quite assured
that anything you write will be accepted. We will pay you,
upon acceptance, anywhere from $1,000 to $5,000 per article
depending upon length. We've always been admirers of your
work . . . By the bye, did you know that one of our associate
editors, Virginia McAnally, sat next to you in English II at the
University of . . . ?"*

So, the man who has kept his style and his energy and his
truth strictly within the Art-form is suddenly visited by wealth.
He is offered readings at Universities from $5000 plus expenses
to 2 grand plus expenses plus whatever he wishes to fuck if he is
still sober enough to do so after the reading or after the party . . .
It is most difficult to a man who has been hated by his landlady in
an 8 dollar a week room to turn away from the easy way. Where
before he had been a pure Artist saying it properly out of pain and
madness and truth, now everybody is willing to listen to his babble
when he no longer has anything to say. A name. A *name*! That's
all they want. And a beard if possible. The American Artist, so
far as I know, with the exception of Jeffers and Pound, has always
taken the bait. No names come to my mind immediately. But name-
calling proves nothing. It happens! They are tricked and trapped,
and, finally, though they don't realize it, they will be thrown away.
Because it was their original energy and truth that enticed the subnormal crowd anyhow . . .

I doubt that this is exactly what you wanted, Norm. I am
hooked on my own cod-fish soul and do not claim exceptionality,
although I probably have it, say, in my own certain fishy-way. When
I'm hired to work as a staff writer for *The New Yorker,* I'll let you
know. Until then, balls away, bung-ho, and I sit here with all different colors of shoe polish . . . whoever breaks in here first, I'm with

him . . . dab it on . . . I've got every color, every shade . . . oh wait, there's one missing . . . oh, shit, I've got *that* already . . .

Luck with your guru issue. I think it's going to be very dull and pontifical, however . . . all those mouths saying anything and everything. well, you asked for it.

1971

[To Lawrence Ferlinghetti]
January 8, 1971

while you run around the country with Corso and Ginsberg, giving readings at the univercities and fucking all the young co-eds and while *I* lay up here creating Art, things happen . . . oh, forgive me, I didn't mean to infer that Ginsberg fucked any chicks. I know he's on the ecology trip and . . . look, I heard from a guy who is supposed to pay these fab. advances on books of short stories . . . so I sent him a few samples and I am supposed to hear soon, but my guess is that the answer will be "no." I believe that he will be scared of my stuff, so let's see. O.K.? I'd really like to see somebody do a book of my new stories, and I think this guy is going to chicken out . . . so I'll be knocking on your door soon with my bag of slimy greasy evil motherfuck stories . . . we have plenty of possibilities of getting together on SOMETHING, jesus christ, it would appear so . . .

[To Steve Richmond]
March 1971

o.k. good on *Post Office,* that it went down for you. I tried to keep some PACE in there. most novels bore me, even the great ones. no pace. I like swifter flowing rivers. o.k.

yeh, *Metamorphosis* is fascinating. no, Kafka, I don't think delves much on the ladies; he is good for where he gets, though. Jeffers, of course, lived through the bloodstream, so he was able to get inside of women and see out of them as they see—something that I have as yet been unable to do, perhaps will never be able to do. D. H. Lawrence never got there, reputation be damned. he just had this one big rather mother-cow and it all come to him through the mother cow—I rather guess Lawrence was a breast-man rather than a leg-man—anyhow, he had his COW and it all transferred through the cow, all the meanings the shades the messages, so he didn't get it quite right. one cow: one message.

[To Lawrence Ferlinghetti]
April 22, 1971

Thanks for card. I am all steamed-up on the book, YOW! couldn't sleep last night so sat up sorting through *Open Cities,* most of them the large format that was issued after *Notes* (the book) came out . . . with these, flipping through, I have discovered story after story after story. Good shit, Larry. Before I get through the stack WE ARE GOING TO HAVE BETWEEN 25 and 50 MORE STORIES! The *wildest* shit since Boccaccio and Swift! You just don't KNOW what you've stumbled on, man. You're gonna get credit for being the greatest editor of the ages. First *Howl,* now this. You'll see. [. . .]

Excuse my enthusiasm. But this is going to be a bomb, this is going to be the end of the moon. by jacking-off Christ, yes. I have to read at S. C. tomorrow and do a little bit of fucking over the weekend, but sometime next week all these other stories are going to land on you. joyful reading. [. . .]

O.K., the book is a flame taller than the sky!

We will advance and forsake stupid realities and drab unrealities bang bang!

All fish will fly, all birds will swim, the lake will be onion soup and the blood will never die.

Bukowski sent Ferlinghetti the two blurbs below; Ferlinghetti used the first one on the back cover of Erections, Ejaculations, Exhibitions and General Tales of Ordinary Madness, *while the second blurb has not been printed before. The projected book of poems and prose,* Bukowskiana, *never took place and it eventually became* Erections.

[To Lawrence Ferlinghetti]
December 30, 1971

Thanks for the letter and the order pamphlet . . . I guess *Bukowskiana* is for real. I am still plenty up and excited on the book. I really believe it will be my best one.

Yes, the photo on front is all right. On the back . . . well, I don't know. By the way, it's "King of the hard-mouth poets . . ." If you want to use that, it's up to you. I did most of my writing for *Open City* . . . referring to the pamphlet. very little, if any, for the *L.A. Free Press* . . . I don't know of any hotshot quotes we might use . . . I'm tired of the one about Sartre and Genet calling me the best poet in America. I don't know how that one ever got started. I doubt the truth of it, I think it was something Jon Webb blew up out of proportion and others picked it up. I don't know.

If you want something for the book back, I can give you a rough rundown:

Charles Bukowski, born 8-16-20, Andernach, Germany. Brought to America at the age of 2. 18 or 20 books of prose and poetry. Bukowski, after publishing prose in *Story* and *Portfolio*, stopped writing for ten years. He arrived in the charity ward of the L.A. County General Hospital, hemorrhaging as a climax to this ten year drinking bout. Some say he didn't die. After leaving the hospital he got a typewriter and began writing again—this time, poetry.

He later returned to prose and gained some fame with his column "Notes of a Dirty Old Man," which he wrote mainly for the paper *Open City*. After 14 years in the Post Office he resigned at the age of 50, he says, to keep from going insane. He now claims to be unemployable and eats typewriter ribbons. Once married, once divorced, many times shacked, he has a 7 year old daughter . . . These dirty and immoral stories appeared mainly in the underground newspapers with *Nola Express* leading in the publication of them. Others have appeared in *The Evergreen Review, Knight, Adam, Pix* and *Adam Reader*. With Bukowski, the votes are still coming in. There seems no middle ground—people either seem to love him or hate him. Tales of his own life and doings are as wild and weird as the very stories he writes. In a sense, Bukowski is a legend in his time . . . a madman, a recluse, a lover . . . tender, vicious . . . never the same . . . these are exceptional stories that come pounding out of his violent and depraved life . . . horrible and holy . . . you cannot read them and ever come away the same again.

Well, Lawrence . . . something like that . . . I don't know . . . What do you think?

[Second blurb]
"A Dictionary of Madness and Sorrow"
Erections, Ejaculations, Exhibitions and General Tales of Ordinary Madness
By Charles Bukowski

No book at City Lights has inflamed as much excitement since Ginsberg's *Howl* as this just released jumbo volume of Bukowski stories—478 pages. Bukowski is the Dostoyevsky of the '70's. Bukowski doesn't only write stories—his whole maniacal and loving soul is embedded in them. The writing is raw but pure laughter through pain. Many of these stories are love stories but hardly common love stories. This is writing from the blood and soul of agony rather than from the intellect. Bukowski also writes of tragedy with humor—the blood-stained cities, the lonely walls, the loves that didn't work are often approached through a comical grace that is almost saintly. There might even be hatred and/or indecency in some of these tales but Bukowski is a gambler—he never strains to please, either in person or in his work. Charles Bukowski is said to be one of the best poets of our time by many of our critics. This book of stories is also an event in our time—acts of horror and genius by a 51-year-old man who has remained quietly hidden from the literati for years and who still remains an isolationist and an enigma . . . If you want to attend this curious circus, this black mass with love bolted across a doorway of beercans.

1972

In the August 4, 1972 issue of Nola Express, *Alta, poet and publisher of the feminist press Shameless Hussy Press, admitted to being "shocked & hurt" by Bukowski's "rape fantasies"—published by Fife in* Nola Express.

[To Darlene Fife]
August 13, 1972

Your Alta is confused. There are men who rape and men who think of rape. Writing of this does not mean that the author condones rape, even if it is written in the first person. The right of creation is the right to mention what does exist. I even know some women—personally—whose greatest desire is to be raped. Creation is creation. For instance, just because a man is black does not mean he can't be a son of a bitch and just because a woman is a woman does not mean she can't be a bitch. Let's not censor ourselves out of reality from a goody-goody stance. Also, from what Alta quotes from my column I can see that she is so fiercely righteous (almost akin to the religious maniac) that she misses the point of the whole thing—that I am poking fun at the male attitude toward the female. I'm sorry that Alta has suffered on the marriage bed (as she mentioned). But let me remind the dear girl that *men* also suffer on the marriage bed. Sometimes *they* are the ones who are doing the service. Really. I might say that Alta is a female chauv. pig. Men are also looking for women who are able to accept love. Prejudice works in all directions. But it's almost useless to counter an attack like Alta's. It will only goad her into a more goody-goody wrong direction. But, still, sometimes these types must be answered. You know, they used to say, how can a person who loves pets, children and dogs be a bad person? Now it is, how can a person who is against war, dirty water, dirty air, how can a person who is fighting for women's rights be a bad person? Or, it used to be, he has long hair and a beard, he's all right. Well, shit, you see, it can all be a stance . . . I reserve the right to create in any manner that reality or humor or even—whim—dictates. All right.

[To William Packard]
October 13, 1972

this writing of poetry, we have to play it loose. I'm glad I can work in a little prose and drinking and woman-fighting to break off the sting. I get into those craft interviews sometimes and I feel like those people are polishing mahogany. I suppose it comes from studying too hard and living too little. Hemingway lived hard but got locked in his craft too and after a while his craft became a cage and killed him. I suppose it's all a matter of feeling your way through. it's like the mirrors we used to get lost in on the places on the pier when we were kids. it's easy enough to lose it all, to get lost. and I'm not talking from any high place either. let's have a beer for luck and hope the ladies still love our wrinkled souls and withering thighs, o, how poetic. shit.

more poems enclosed. I'm trying to build a stockpile and I will blow the world up with my poems. yeh.

[To David Evanier]
Late 1972

[. . .] I've never much liked writing, creation, I mean what the other boys have done. it seemed to me rather thin and pretensive, still does. I kept writing not because I felt I was so good but because I felt they were so bad, including Shakespeare, all those. the stilted formalism, like chewing cardboard. I didn't feel very good when I was 16, 17, 18, I walked into the libraries and there was nothing to read. I searched all the rooms, all the books. then I walked back out on the streets and I saw the first face, the buildings, the automobiles, whatever was being said had nothing to do with what I was seeing before my eyes, it was a mimic, a farce. there was no help. Hegel, Kant . . . some fucker called Andre Gide . . . names, names, and build-ups. Keats, what a bag of shit. nothing helped. I began to see something in Sherwood Anderson. He almost got there, he was clumsy and stupid, *but* he let you fill in the blanks. unforgivable. Faulkner was phoney as greased wax. Hemingway got close early, then started strumming and turning this big machine which kept farting in your face. Celine wrote one immortal book which made me laugh for nights and days (*Journey*), then he got into housewife petty bitching. Saroyan. he, like Hem, knew the importance of the root and the clear word, the easy and natural line, but Saroyan, knowing the line, kid, he lied: he said: BEAUTIFUL, BEAUTIFUL, and it wasn't BEAUTIFUL. I wanted to hear what it was, all the chickenshit fears, the worries, the madness; fuck the grand stance. I couldn't find it. I drank and screwed, went crazy in bars, smashed windows, got the shit beaten out of me, lived. I didn't know what. I'm still working. I don't have it right yet. I probably won't get it right. I even love my ignorance. I love my yellow butter-smeared belly of ignorance. I lick my god damn soul out with my typewriter tongue. I don't entirely want art. I want entertainment, first. I want to forget. I want a buzzing, some shouting among the wine-dizzy chandeliers. I want. I mean, if we can work art *in* after we become *interested,* fine. but let's not get holy, tra la, tra la.

[To Steve Richmond]
December 24, 1972

[. . .] you've got your right to criticize me and much of it is probably correct, but one thing you're going to learn, finally, I feel is that creation is not photography or even necessarily standard truth. creation carries its own truth or lie and only the years can name which it is. what people don't understand is that although something *seems* to be about them it isn't necessarily about them, it can be a portion of them—that moment—and a portion of all men moulded into something that must be said. I've read some poems that *seemed* to be about me, being called Bullshitski and other things, but I had to laugh because I knew it wasn't the entire picture.

I think sometimes we can become too holy and therefore, caged.

I believe that you will find your publisher some day, and perhaps the later that comes the better it will be for you. meanwhile, please don't feel you're being knifed. anything I have to say to you or about you or about anybody else will never be secretive, it will always be out front.

you've got your right to feel down sometimes, I don't blame you. but it didn't come easy for me, still doesn't. like I say, let's do our WORK. you have too much talent and honesty, I'd rather not be your enemy, don't make me into one.

1973

Bukowski put Robert Creeley down in a poem titled "on Creeley" published in a little magazine in 1971.

[To Michael Andre]
March 6, 1973

[. . .] I no longer hate Creeley. he has worked hard on a certain type of form of writing that I don't understand. but he has put his energy and his life into it. he's going to take a great many knocks. he has probably taken so many that it has become ingrained for him to be feisty about it. a man has to fight back finally or the slime worms will dominate. I didn't mean to be a slime worm against Creeley. I was cheap. I just got my back up without making a true study of him. it's just the standard knock (automatic) against top dog or dogs or limelight. it's cheap and I should have known better. but I am a slow grower, M. If I die at the age of 80 I will probably be 14 years old. do you understand something of what I am trying to say? o.k. then.

———————

[To Robert Head and Darlene Fife]
May 23, 1973

Here's another submission. Listen, I know what you mean, but *Notes of a Human Being* is just too precious. *Notes of a Dirty Old Man* takes the pressure off and allows me to say more. Probably, in history, more harm was done by guys thinking they were human beings than any other sort. I mean, let's steer from the holy and maybe with a little luck we might get holy. Strain or dedication doesn't seem to do it.

Besides, good and evil, right and wrong keep changing; it's a climate rather than a law (moral). I'd rather stay with the climates. I think that's what a lot of revolutionaries fail to see about my work: I'm more revolutionary than they are. It's only that they've been taught too much. The first process of learning or creation is the undoing of teaching. To do this it's much easier to be a dirty old man than a human being, all right? fine, how are you today?

[To Darlene Fife]
[?June] 1973

Yes, the problem of working for the govt. or accepting a grant from the govt . . . the problem of staying alive, somehow, for a while. I've heard the arguments.

I'm not a true revolutionary. I just write words down. But the idea of replacing one govt. with another govt. hardly seems a major gain to me. we've got to begin with the individual. we've got to replace the individual we've got now with another type, or if we can't do that we've got to patch him up a bit anyhow. and I don't have the answers to that. more words, probably. words, words, words, words. the building of the flow.

in one area all of us fail badly. the man-woman relationship. I've seen more bad faith and lacking and inconsistency in this area than in any about. people just aren't large enough to care truly, and if the male and the female can't find each other then how can they find a government?

ah well, the birds are still singing . . .

Henderson, founder of the Pushcart Press and associate editor at Doubleday at the time, did not get to publish Bukowski's poetry.

[To William Henderson]
July 2, 1973

Of course, it's good that you might be interested in a collection of my poems. However, I have one of these running contracts with Black Sparrow Press, et. al., "your next 3 books . . ." And John Martin runs off book after book and he has been very fair and splendid with me. In fact, my most recent poems have just been gathered and are to appear in the Fall under the title *Burning in Water, Drowning in Flame.*

To be published by Doubleday, however, would be quite an honor and John has said that he will never stand in the way if something good should work toward me. I believe him. He's a very good sort.

What I might suggest is a selected poems edition. I mean we can call it *Selected Poems* but I still might give it a title? And I understand that if I send a manuscript to you that it is just a submission and that it is your holy right to reject it. I have known one or two writers who have misunderstood the workings of this nature and have felt deleted and bungholed because it didn't work. I'm not this way. You can be free with me.

I have never had a *Selected Poems* and I would like to submit to you the best of my poems. It might be a total powerhouse. Then, too, it might be a big god damned yawn. You're the editor.

However, Martin is on vacation, won't be back until July ten, so forth. I'll have to ask him for my freedom when he returns. Have you read my novel *Post Office*? ah, it doesn't interest you? ah well, I understand.

I am living in the house of a young lady and there is sometimes trouble here—she says it's love and I say love is trouble; anyhow, I leave my present address below and also one where I can be reached if somehow love makes me wander and vanish. Very good to hear from you. yes, yes.

[To Rochelle Owens]
September 8, 1973

I saw your poem about me and things in the [*Unmuzzled*] *Ox*, and it's all right, yes, I've been tired of poetry for years, for centuries but I kept writing it because the others were doing it so badly—lavender tresses against the moon's edge—(theatre shit like that), and I still don't even think much about writing it but they still write it so badly, so I grind it on in, the words should rip the paper a bit, make sounds, be simply clear and bold and humorous and suicidal.

o, this is too holy, but you know what I mean.

now I rather flop around all day, I just flop around and the world grinds out there and I've been in so much of that grind but there are some walls here now and I hope the luck holds so I don't have to get ground up some more. I think I've earned my stripes. I think I've earned my legs and my eyes and my typewriter ribbon. lemme have 'em a while.

I'm going out now to eat a hamburger and smoke 3 or 4 cigarettes. somebody is pounding on the stairway with a hammer. there are assholes everywhere. notice this next time you go outside.

you write a pretty good jumping poem.

yes, yes.

Several Nola Express *readers, including poet Clayton Eshleman, asked editors Fife and Head to stop running Bukowski's short stories in* Nola Express.

[To Darlene Fife]
November 8, 1973

[. . .] There are some who think revolution should only be in the streets, not in the Arts. Understand that any new movement forward into the Arts has always (with exceptions) been met with derision and hostility and hatred. Exploration into sexuality or into any area of human maneuverability written down as poem, story or novel does not necessarily mean that I condone the action of the characters involved. Or, on the other hand, it may mean that I condone the action of the characters involved. I have no idea at the time of the writing. I am a feeler, not a thinker. I am often wrong, I write much crap, and the nature of much of my work is a gamble. But all of this allows me a looseness to kick free, and high. I don't claim any special holiness, and I've already said too much. But if the readers of *Nola* want me out I will get out. But I won't go to my psychiatrist to tell him about my bad dreams, I'll go to the harness races next Wednesday night, drink a cheap green beer and bet win on the six horse, ah, lalala lala lalala lalalala la.

1975

A Bukowski short story, illustrated by Robert Crumb, was published in 1975 in Arcade, the Comics Revue, *coedited by Griffith.*

[To Bill Griffith]
June 9, 1975

Sorry I've been so slow in responding but I've been on a split with this woman and my guts are dangling out, all that bit. I'm trying to paste myself back together to get ready from the next war. so, meanwhile, the writing has stalled with all else and I just don't have excessive material. My problem is that I don't get any rejection. Shit, it's awful. Martin has a whole filing cabinet of my stuff though and he might pull something out. He appears to have masses of stuff—like novels begun and not finished, notes from the madhouse and drunk tank, so forth.

Crumb, we know, IZ COMIX. the way he draws his people and the way they step across the page, it holds all this wonderful juice and glow. I met him once at Liza Williams' when I was living with her, and he was one of the most unaffected people I've ever met. It would be a most honorable magic high for me to have him illustrate some of my fucked-up characters. I sure hope something works. and regret my present state of gross and dangle. However, I've outlived other women who have attempted to tack me to the cross and I'll probably get down from this one too.

1978

[To John Martin]
August 29, 1978

Just read your letters to *Wormwood* [*Review*] and *N[ew] Y[ork] Q[uarterly]* and myself. I think you've gotten yourself into too much of a tizzy over nothing. And I also get the feeling that sometimes when you write to me you consider me somewhat of an idiot.

Let's clarify some points as we hit them in your letter. "The books we publish here are really the important part of the whole scene, as that's where your real income is coming from."

Point: my income from you is $500 a month, which amounts to $6,500 a year. Out of this I pay child support, which is nontax deductible. As the big boy of your publishing house I am probably listed in the poverty level and eligible for food stamps, and have been for years. Of course, you know that in former years I've lived off of less, much less. I haven't complained about this because I am crazy enough to just want to sit down to a typewriter and write. But what I do object to is your telling me how well Sparrow and Buk are doing. It's not all that prosperous and never has been, for *me*. I speak here of economics only.

"If I didn't publish your books here first, then there would be no German and French translations." This reminds me much of a statement my father made when I objected going to World War II. "But, my son, if it hadn't been for a war I wouldn't have met your

146

mother and you would not have been born." That, it seems to me, was not a very good pro-war argument. Your statement is not necessarily true. Some of my work was translated and appeared in foreign publications that were never published by Black Sparrow. And, who knows? Someone might have suggested a book translation? This is the importance of appearing in magazines. I think the *main* reason my work has been translated is that, so far, my writing has been strong enough and interesting enough to warrant it.

Marvin Malone has been publishing special editions and centerfolds of writers as a regular feature of his magazine for years. He has done it several times in the past for me and it never bothered you before.

And the reference to a "leash" around Malone's neck . . . my god, please. You ask that I not feel too free about giving away "large chunks of work, as per Malone." John, all writers submit their work to journals as they write it, poets especially, novelists sometimes and short story and article writers, always. There is nothing criminal or foolish about this process. I send large areas of work to *Wormwood* and the *NYQ* because they are the best two poetry journals in existence. I write 5, 6, 7, no, I would say ten times the amount of poetry that the average poet writes. If I divided all the poems into little batches of 4 or 5 and sent them off to every crappy little mag in America I wouldn't have time to write, I'd be pasting up envelopes night and day. I think that you are getting over-possessive and wary. There aren't that many spooks in the bush—you have thousands of poems to choose from and they are still leaping off this typer like crazy.

Then in your letter to Malone you ask for ten of the chapbooks to sell to your customers. I don't think he'll react too well to that. It's like you're looking for every edge. Say like in the 75 (really 150) drawings I do for each book. That takes me a month during which time I can do *nothing* else creative. You sell 75 of these books (signed) for $2625, which, if you subtract it from my $6500 salary leaves you only $3875 to pay me. You've got wet back labor working for you. And once you told me over the phone, "Just think, for every drawing you do, you get $35." That's when I first thought, this man really thinks me an idiot.

"Let me bring out the books."

You are, John. But you're often like a jealous wench.

I remember the projected book of Bukowski-Richmond letters. You went crazy on that one. And Richmond went crazier.

As far as, "the whole secret is to be big enough so that the work gets around and is read by a decent number of people, and yet remain small enough so that the Internal Revenue Service doesn't come around and ask for an accounting of every penny since 1971."

John, if they do, I've got nothing to worry about. I remember once when your office was still in L.A., coming around to do some signings and you said as I walked in, "Here comes the great man, here comes the great writer." O.k. I brought your shipping clerk some beer. Then we got to talking around and your shipping clerk gave you a little sass, and you turned to me and said, "Look at this $90 a week shipping clerk trying to wise it up with me." That sounded pretty good to me because you were paying me between $250 and $300 a month, I forget which. And he wasn't even a famous shipping clerk.

I've stuck with you. I've had offers from New York publishers. I've had offers from competitors. I've stayed with you. People have told me that I was stupid, many people. That hasn't bothered me. I make up my own mind for my own reasons. You were there when nobody else was, you helped me get money through archives. You bought me a good typewriter. Nobody was knocking at my door. I have loyalty. I guess it comes from my German blood. But I ask you to leave my mind clear for my writing; all I want to do is type and drink my wine and do some small things. Letters like this are a waste of energy. Just let me write and mail my shit out like any other writer. Don't be too much of a mother hen. I've lucked it with some good poems this year, plenty of them. I'm glad they are still arriving and swarming all over the place. *Women* is my best work. It's going to cause a great deal of hatred, much reaction, just like any excellent original work of art has always done. Fine. And we should do better in Europe with this work than any other. But I want to go on, I want to write and keep right on doing my act. I just wish you wouldn't treat me always like the complete idiot. *I know what's going on.* That's why I'm able to write it down on paper.

You are just like anybody else I know in my personal life. People have a tendency to guide me around, to pull me around by the nose. Once in a while I have to give them a nip on the hand. My old black cat, Butch, does that once in a while. I understand him more and more. Let's hope that you understand me. It's a long time to 80, if I make it, so let's make the road clear with no bullshit on the path. I want to come to your funeral and be able to drop a tear and a small bouquet of flowers. Ok?

1979

[To Carl Weissner]
January 15, 1979

I hope you haven't started translating *Women* yet. John Martin and I are at it—I claim he has inserted too much of *his* writing into the novel. Some pages enclosed to illustrate. I am having the original script xeroxed and will soon mail to you. John claims I sent over 100 pages of changes to original script. When I get these from him I will mail them on to you. I really feel he has changed my wordage too much, sometimes every other sentence. This is disrespect to me. I don't care about minor changes in grammar and straightening out past and present tense but when too many sentences are fucked with it disturbs the natural flow of my writing. My writing is jagged and harsh, I want it to *remain* that way, I don't want it *smoothed* out. Also large sections of the novel have been eliminated. When you get the total manuscript you will be able to choose what you want in or out. This way your choice is narrowed; I mean the way the novel reads now.

John claims innocence and is going to come down and we are going to go over the whole thing. He told me that sometimes the typist gets tired and throws something in. His typist must have been tired all the way through the novel.

Anyhow, the enclosures are *minor* changes that were not in the original script I have on hand. I hope you have not begun translating. I asked John, "Would you have done this with William Faulkner?" And he certainly wouldn't have done it with a college professor and *not* with Creeley, not even with a comma. I guess it is my coming out of the lower working class, bumland, that makes him think I don't quite know what I'm doing. But *instinctively* I do and he should realize this. Can you imagine him touching up a Van Gogh? Well, shit . . .

Linda Lee and I send hellos of love to you and Mikey and Waltraut.

p.s.—I wonder what the Frenchies and Italians will think? Looks like I gotta mail them off copies of original script plus the 100 pages of changes. It's a good novel now but I feel it would have been a great and a wild novel without the bad writing inserted and the other parts left out. Instead of the centuries getting something great they're just getting this milked-down and walked over version . . .

[To John Fante]
January 31, 1979

Thanks for the good letter. It's a very odd, a very strange feeling to get a letter from you. It has been some decades since I first read *Ask the Dust*. Martin has sent me a xerox of the novel and I am starting in on it again and it reads as well as ever. Along with Dos's *Crime and Punishment* and Celine's *Journey* it is my favorite novel. Forgive me for not answering sooner but right now I am into a great many things: screenplay, correcting somebody else's screenplay, a short story and also drinking and playing the horses and fighting with my girlfriend, and visiting my daughter, and then feeling bad and then feeling good, and all the rest of it. Then I lost your letter and I was so proud of it and last night I found it, I had been using the back of the envelope to make suggestions on for corrections on this fellow's screenplay (and adaptation of my first novel *Post Office*). So here it is raining and I am writing you rapidly because I want to get down to the bank to cash this check so I can make the racetrack tomorrow.

Your writing helped my life, gave me real hope that a man could just put the words down and let the emotions ride out. Nobody has done this as well as you have. I am going to read the book slowly, enjoy it once again and hope that I can write a reasonable foreword. [H. L.] Mencken had a good eye, among other things, and I think it is time that a talent like yours surfaced again, even though Black Sparrow is not New York it has some prestige and bangbang and such books are more apt to last and to be read by other people than the general public which simply eats up whatever New York feeds them.

Great to hear from you, Fante, you're number one all the way. Forgive my typing. After I finish the book and do the foreword I will mail it to you for your o.k., hopefully. Best to your wife and son. The sky is wet today and tomorrow the track will be muddy but I will be thinking of you and the luck that I will have of being able to tell people why *Ask the Dust* is so good. Thank you, yes, yes, yes . . .

———————

[To Carl Weissner]
February 6, 1979

[. . .] on *Women*, the 100 pages of corrections are lost somewhere. Some of it evidently did get in . . . for instance at the end I gave the cat black fur and yellow eyes . . . Anyhow, it's quite a mess-up and I guess John Martin just kind of went crazy. I think it was a pretty shameful thing to do—work in his "writing," I mean. I guess we all go crazy now and then. Anyhow, the 2nd printing will read better. I guess when people compare the 2 editions they'll never know the real story. They will be more apt to think that I went addled with senility and somebody else went ahead and made the changes for me. It's pretty tough to take because I don't mind being criticized for my own writing but to be laid open for somebody else's isn't so good. Anyhow, I will have to keep a closer watch on John in future work of mine. I doubt that he will fuck me up again. Sometimes I get rather sickened by some of Martin's acts and methods. I wish you were my god damned editor, but thank the gods at least that I have you for a translator, agent, and friend. (oh yeah, John actually said, "Sometimes the typist gets bored and throws in something." Wonder if Faulkner and J. Joyce were bothered with that?) [. . .]

I'm into the film script [*Barfly*] with Barbet [Schroeder], 30 or so pages; but I'm surprised—he wants a *plot* and an evolvement of character. shit, my characters seldom evolve, they are too fucked-up. they can't even type. I like to let it go free and sometimes there is nothing to explain about them, they are just jagged edges of something. I don't mind a few hints on how movies should be but when somebody starts working the strings on my puppets they often forget to dance, forget how to do anything. ah well, ah well.

———————

[To John Fante]
December 2, 1979

It was good to hear the end of your novel over the phone; it was more Fante all over again, top grade, the only grade as always. It lifted the hell out of me to know that you were still doing it. You were my main charge to begin with and you are charging me all over again after all these years.

I've been in an impotent period and I haven't had many of those. I don't mean that my writing has always been exceptional, what I mean is that it has always kept coming. It has stopped of late. Well, a few poems the other night but it hasn't seemed the same. I've found myself snapping at Linda and I even kicked the cat the other night. I don't like to act like a little prima d. but it looks like if the stuff doesn't come out I get poisoned, I forget how to laugh, I find myself no longer listening to my symphony music on the radio and when I look into the mirror I see a very mean man there, tiny eyes, yellow face—I'm pinched-in, useless, a dry fig. I mean, when the writing goes, what is there, what's left? Routine. Routine motions. Flapjack thoughts. I can't face that stale dance.

Hearing from you, having Joyce read me the end of your novel, hearing the Fante lilt of courage and passion has boosted me out of my deadness. The wine is open and the radio is on and I am going to stick some sheets into this machine and it will come again, because of you. It will come because of Celine and Dos and Hamsun but mainly because of you. I don't know where you got it but the gods certainly stuffed you with it. You have meant, do mean more to me than any man living or dead. I had to tell you this. Now I am beginning to smile a little. Thank you, Arturo [Bandini].

1980

[To John Martin]
[?June] 1980

[. . .] Henry Miller. I didn't feel much when he went because I've been expecting it. What I liked is that when he was going he went to paint and what I've seen of his things are very good, warm, hot color. Not many lives like his. In his writing he did the thing, like that, when nobody else was going it, doing it. He cracked the hard black walnut. I always had trouble reading him because he would leave off into this Star-Trek contemplation sperm-jizz babble but it made the good parts better when you finally got to them, but frankly, I usually gave up most of the time. Lawrence was different, he was solid all the way through but Miller was more modern, less artsy, until he got into his Star-Trek babbling. I think a problem Miller caused (and it's not his fault) is that when he hustled and pushed his stuff (early) he has made others think that that's the way it is done, so now we have these battalions of semi-writers knocking on doors and hustling and proclaiming their genius because they have been "undiscovered" and that the very fact of non-discovery makes them sure of their genius because "the world is not ready for them yet."

For most of them the world will never be ready; they don't know how to write, they are simply not touched by the grace of the word or the way. Not those I have met or read. I hope there are others. We need them. It's pretty fallow, around. But even like those who come around with their guitars, I've found that the least talented scream the loudest, are the most abusive and the most self-assured. They've slept on my couches and puked on my rugs and drank my drinks and they have told me, continuously, of their greatness. I'm not a publisher of songs or poems or novels and/ or short stories. The battlefield has an address; to beg of friends or girlfriends or others is masturbation against the sky. Yes, I'm drinking very much wine tonight and I guess I'm dizzied with the visitors. Writers, please save me from the writers; the conversation of the Alvarado street whores was much more interesting, and more original. [. . .]

Henry Miller. A damn good soul. He liked Celine like I like Celine. Like I told Neeli Cherry, "the secret is in the line." And I meant one line at a time. Lines containing factories, and a shoe on its side next to a beercan in a hotel room. Everything is here, it flashes back and forth. They are not going to beat us, not even the graves. The joke is ours; we pass through in high style; there's nothing that they can do with us.

[To Mike Gold]
November 4, 1980

I know of another editor who was going to put out a "rejection" issue, printing the rejected material and the writers' thoughts on such. I didn't send him anything, telling him that I thought my rejected stuff should have been rejected.

The issue never came out. I suppose when the ed got the rejected material and the complaints of the writers spread out that he had a little house of inbred horrors.

Of course, there's much bad material published in large circulation mags and littles, and in books. Bad editors will continue to edit and bad writers will continue to write. Much publishing is done through politics, friends and natural stupidity. What little good writing does come out is largely accidental, or a mathematical rarity: when a good writer knocks into a good editor.

To encourage bad writers to continue writing in spite of rejection doesn't matter: they're going to do it anyhow. The little mags print about 15% of material that is fair writing; the larger mags, perhaps 20.

Sad things happen in the little mag field. I knew a writer who was writing fairly live stuff for the littles. He got published here and there, there and here. He had 2 or 3 chapbooks published by little press editors, say issues of 200. This writer had a terrible job and he came home each night, his guts stamped and dangling, and he wrote it down. A chapbook or 2 more, many appearances in the littles—every time you opened a mag, here was his name. He decided he was a writer, came west with wife and kids, wife got job and he sat over the typer and punched at it. His bookcase was full of little mags and chapbooks and he gave poetry readings to crowds of 9 or 11, where they passed the hat. His poetry gradually softened but his bookcase was behind him. Of course it couldn't pay the electric bill, but since he was a genius there was the wife to do that, get that bill and all the others and the rent and so forth. I hope he's working again. Maybe it's time for his wife to sit down to the typer. This is one case but I believe it could be multiplied by 50 or 1,000.

It's confusing as to what's real or what isn't real. I remember when I was in my early twenties, living on one candy bar a day so I could have time to write, I was writing 5 or 6 short stories a week and they were all coming back. But when I read the *New Yorker,* *Harper's,* the *Atlantic,* I couldn't detect anything in there but 19th century literature, careful and contrived, worked out tediously, inch by inch of boredom crawling across the pages, name writers, fakers, yawning me into imbecility. I had an idea I was a pretty good writer but there was no way of knowing, I couldn't spell and my grammar was crap (they still are) but I felt I was doing something better than they were: I was starving excellently.

Because you're not accepted doesn't necessarily mean you're a genius. Maybe you just write badly. I know of some who publish their own books who point to the 2 or 3 examples of great writers of the past who also did that. Ow. They also point to guys who weren't recognized in their lifetime (Van Gogh and co.), and that means, of course, that . . . Ow.

The rejects from the big mags are usually printed and therefore soulless. But I've gotten some things from little mag editors who thought they were gods. One I remember: "Just what the fuck is this shit?" No signature, just the large ink scrawl across the page. Much more than once, things of this nature. How do I know it's not from some 17 year old kid with acne, hooked on Yeats, using his father's discarded mimeo machine in his garage? I know: read the mag. Who wants to? When you're writing 30 poems a month there's no time to read. If there's time, and some money, you drink.

Very successful writers are like presidents: they get the vote because the madding crowd recognizes something of itself in them.

It's confusing, Mike, I don't know what to tell you. I'm getting ready to go out and play the quarter horses.

1981

[To Carl Weissner]
February 23, 1981

[. . .] I should be getting back into the short story after I finish *Ham* [*on Rye*]. *Ham* has been harder and slower than the other novels because where I didn't have to be careful with the other novels, I have to be careful here. That childhood, growing up stuff has been painful for most of us to do, go through, and there is a tendency to make too much of it. I've read very little literature about that stage of life that didn't make me a little bit sick because of its preciousness. I am trying to luck it into the balance, like maybe the horror of the hopelessness can create some slight background laughter, even if it comes from the throat of the devil. [. . .]

Reading the letters of Hemingway. Awful stuff. At least in the early letters. He's quite a politician. Playing with, meeting the powers that be. Well, maybe it was all right? There weren't so many writers then. Or magazines. Or books. Or things. Now there are hundreds of thousands of writers and thousands of lit mags and many publishers and many critics, but mainly, hundreds of thousands of writers. Say you call a plumber nowadays. He'll come over with his pipe wrench in one hand, his plunger in the other and a small chapbook of his selected madrigals in one of his asshole pockets. Even see a kangaroo in the zoo, he'll eye you and then pull a sheath of pomes from his pouch, typewritten, single-spaced on waterproof 8 and one half by eleven.

———————

The play discussed below, called Bukowski, We Love You, *was premiered in Rome in 1981. Galiano produced* Storie di ordinaria follia [Tales of Ordinary Madness], *directed by Marco Ferreri in 1981.*

[To John Martin]
February 24, 1981

You've probably gotten something from Silvia Bizio about wanting rights to about half the Black Sparrow Bukowski books in your arsenal to put into a god damned play. They offer no $$$ and claim to be a little non-profit outfit but actually they are going to run this thing for two years in many different cities. I hope you didn't give your o.k. but if you have . . . well, they aren't clear on the rest of the steal which are many stories from City Lights books.

Bizio has been bugging me constantly to sign away these rights. I did an interview for her and also let her do a bit on video with me spouting off about various nothings. But I've personally taken a dislike to her as a person and to her ways. She's evidently fronting for these crooks and I've told her I want nothing to do with the whole scene.

"But they've been preparing this for two years!"

"They love you!"

"They want to pay your fare to come and see them and their play."

I told her, "That's balls! Why didn't they try to get permission before starting out?"

I don't like the Italians, they're sneaks, their whole way of doing things makes me sick. How can they just steal my work and put it on stage without asking? [Sergio] Galiano is trying to make a *movie* out of some of the same stories. If *he* pays, where do they get off?

And then there's another problem, Galiano. Supposed to pay $44,000, he has sent 4,000 and claims the other money was wired over a month ago. Nothing but a lie. And he's down in *Georgia* with Ben Gazzara, shooting the films now. The Italians . . . Hitler didn't trust them either and I can see why, they slide and lie and trick.

I'm sure the same thing has happened to other writers. A writer is only looked at as a guy who puts words down on paper. He's an easy take. He's only thinking of the next line and doesn't want to be bothered with externals that don't fit his little mood-state. Which is true but he also doesn't like to get raped.

The bastards also know the cost of court procedure and that they can flee and hide in some Italian hamlet, giving us the big finger.

Ah well, John, a couple of poems enclosed.

1982

[To John Martin]
January 3, 1982

Well, we're past all their fake crap again, and as they resort to their dull normalcy we can get to it.

Writing has never been work to me, and even when it comes out badly, I like the action, the sound of the typer, a way to go. And even when I write badly and it comes back, I look at it and I don't mind too much: I've got a chance to improve. There's the matter of staying with it, tapping away, it seems to keep mending together; the mistakes and the good luck until it sounds and reads and feels better. Not that it's important or not important. Just tap tap tap. Of course, in the typing it's good if something comes along that is interesting to say, and such things don't arrive every day. You've got to wait a couple of days sometimes. And you've got to know that the big boys who have been doing it for centuries really haven't done it too well, even though you have copied from them, couldn't have started at any beginning without them, there's still nothing to owe. So, tap tap tap . . .

Well, I hope that you and I hold together a little longer. It's been a magic journey and you've gone about your business and I've gone about mine and there's been very little trouble between us. I think we are both out of the old time school where things are done in a certain way and we keep doing them that way; which means we mix the best of modernity with the best of the past—the 30's and 40's and maybe even a peek of the 20's. I think the main thing the new ones lack is the grand eternal style, a method of approach, a method of battling pain and success. We're pretty good, John. Let's stay in there. Round eleven coming up, and I think the fucker on the other stool is getting tired.

Dangling in the Tournefortia *was reviewed by Peter Schjeldahl for* The New York Times Book Review *in January 1982.*

[To Carl Weissner]
February 13, 1982

[. . .] My critic at the *N. Y. Times* is probably a nice enough fellow, knows his language, well read, so on. Don't think he ever missed a meal, though, or broke a leg or got pissed on by a whore, or ever slept on a park bench, and so forth. Not that these things are necessary, they happen, but when they do you tend to think a bit differently. I myself like *Dangling*. I think I am getting a better and better feel for the WORD after all these years without losing too much of the madness. *Ham on Rye* I like best. Martin claims it's the best thing I've ever written. "It has all the guts and grits of the 19th century Russian masters." Well, that would be nice. I really liked those boys. They could wade through the dismal agony, kind of laughing out of the sides of their mouths.

[To Jack Stevenson]
March 1982

[. . .] Most of them begin the same way. The Poets, I mean. They start fairly good. They are isolated and they come down on the words because they are more or less startled out of their minds, they're innocent, you see. There's some whiff to them in the beginning. Then they start making it. They give more and more readings, they meet others of their ilk. They talk to each other. They begin to feel as if they have brains. They make statements on government, soul, homosexuality, organic gardening . . . so forth . . . They know about everything but plumbing and they ought to know about that because they load it with shit. It's really disheartening to see them evolve. Trips to India, breathing exercises—they improve their lungs so they can talk it up more. Soon they are *teachers,* they are standing before other people telling them *how to do it.* Not just how to *write* but how to do *everything.* They get sucked into every available trap. These once fairly original souls most often become the very thing or things they were fighting against in the first place. And you ought to see them read: they LOVE it, the audience, the little coeds, the little boys, that whole convent of idiots that attends poetry readings—icecream threads of people with jelly assholes and Chinese noodle brains (soft). How they love to read, these poets. How they love to let their voices waft. "Now," they say, "I'm only going to read 3 more poems!" Like, I mean, what the hell, who cares? And of course, the 3 poems are longies. And I'm not generalizing: one is just like the other in this way. There are minor differences: some are black, some are homo. Some are black and homo. But they're all dull. And I'm a nazi. Sure. Recall me.

My idea of a writer is somebody who writes. Who sits at a typewriter and puts the words down. That would appear to be the essence. Not to teach others how, not to sit in seminars, not to read to the madding crowd. Why are these such extroverts? If I had wanted to be an actor I would have tried for the Hollywood cameras. Of the half hundred writers I've met one way or the other, only two seemed to me to be the least bit human. One I've met 3 or 4 times—he's blind with both legs amputated, 72 years old, he continues to write, and well, dictating to his wonderful wife while on his deathbed. The other is a crazy and natural one who types his stuff in Mannheim, Germany.

Otherwise, the last one I want to drink with or listen to is a writer. I've found more gut-life in old newsboys, in janitors, in the kid waiting window at the all-night taco stand. It seems to me that writing draws the worst, not the best, it seems to me that the printing presses of the world are just endlessly pressing out the pulp of insufficient souls which insufficient critics call literature, poetry, prose. It's useless, except for maybe that single bright spark, now and then, which seldom holds, knows how.

As I get into the 2nd bottle of wine and glance back over this letter I will note that if it is ever seen that some reference will be made that Bukowski mentioned Blacks and Homosexuals as if he might have a distaste for them. Therefore, let me mention: women, Mexicans, lesbians, Jews.

Let me state, that my distaste is for Humanity and especially, the creative writer. This is not only the age of Hydrogen doom, it is also the age of Fear, Immense Fear.

I don't like Whitey either. And I am Whitey.

What do I like? I like getting into this 2nd bottle of wine. Got to clean up the day. Lost ten dollars at the track today. What a useless thing. Rather like jacking-off into a stack of dripping hotcakes.

I've always rather admired the Chinese. I suppose that's because most of them are so far away.

The short story "The Hog" remains unpublished.

[To Carl Weissner]
May 29, 1982

Ham on Rye was hard to sit down to, to write the first word down. After that, it got easier. I think I had the distance to bring it off. I thought about it a month or so before I began. After all, who wants to read childhood stuff? It brings out the worst kind of writing.

I hoped to bring in the sense of the ridiculous and some humor.

My parents were strange. Oh, yes. It's not in the book but once when I came in from the bum weighing 139 pounds they charged me room, board and laundry. Maybe I put that in *Factotum*. I don't remember.

I'm back to playing with the poem now. Although *Hustler* recently asked me for a short story so I sat down and typed them a ditty called "The Hog." I liked their reject: ". . . the subject matter is just too strong for us to handle. Specifically, it's the bestiality and also its violent result that we don't feel we can accept."

So I popped it off to German *Playboy*. It should make them shit up a raw *wiener schnitzel* but I expect it back.

1983

[To Loss Pequeño Glazier]
February 16, 1983

I don't know exactly how it works. What I mean is, I'm not writing much better now than I was decades ago when I was starving to death in those small rooms and on those park benches and in those flophouses, and while I was being nearly murdered in those factories and in the post office. Durability has something to do with it: I've outlived many of the editors who rejected me, and some of the women too. If there is any difference in my writing now, I feel more entertained when I write it. But things happen very quickly—one moment you're a drunken bum fighting with drunken and drugged and insane women in a low-class apartment, then it seems the next thing you're in Europe and you walk into a hall and there are 2,000 wild people waiting for you to read some poems. And you're 60 years old . . .

Now I'm headed toward 63 and I don't have to give readings to get the wine and the rent. If I had wanted to be an actor, I would have been one. Posturing before the crowd is not my idea of getting it off. I get my offers. Recently heard from a nice fellow who also wrote me last year: ". . . some of the people who have already accepted are John Updike, Czeslaw Milosz, Stephen Spender, Edmund White, Jonathan Miller, Dick Cavett, and Wendell Berry. So, you see, you'd be in good company . . ."

I told him, no. Although the "honorarium" was plenty.

Why do these people have to do this?

Well, anyhow, what I'm trying to say is, for me, having enough money at the moment allows me to live in this small town, San Pedro, where the people are quite normal and easy and dull and good and you'd have a hard time finding a writer or a painter or an actor anywhere around. This is where I can live with my 3 cats and drink almost every night and type until 2 or 3 a.m. And the next day there's the race track. That's all I need. And trouble will always find you (me). There are still good and unhappy moments with the female. But I like the set-up. I'm glad I'm not Norman Mailer or Capote or Vidal, or Ginsberg reading with The Clash, and I'm glad I'm not The Clash.

What I'm getting at is that when Luck comes your way you can't let it Swallow you. Getting famous when you're in your twenties is a very difficult thing to overcome. When you get half-famous when you're over 60, it's easier to make adjustments. Old Ez Pound used to say, "Do your *work*." And I knew exactly what he meant. Even though to me writing is never work no more than drinking is. And, of course, I'm drinking now and so if this gets a little muddled, well, that's my *style*.

I don't know, you know. Take some poets. Some start very well. There is a flash, a burning, a gamble in their way of putting it down. A good first or second book, then they seem to *d i s s o l v e*. You look around and they are teaching CREATIVE WRITING at some university. Now they think they know how to WRITE and they are going to tell others how to. This is a sickness: they have accepted themselves. It's unbelievable that they can do this. It's like some guy coming along and trying to tell me how to fuck because he thinks he fucks good.

If there are any good writers, I don't think these writers go around, walk around, talk around, abound, thinking, "I am a writer." They live because there's nothing else to do. It piles up: the horrors and the non-horrors and the conversations, the flat tires and the nightmares, the screamings, the laughters and the deaths and the long spaces of zero and all that, it begins to total and then they see the typer and they sit down and it pushes out, there's no planning, it occurs: if they are still lucky.

There aren't any rules. I can no longer read other writers. I am a loner. But I borrow from others in my spaces of nil. I like a good professional football game or a boxing match or a horse race where all the contenders are nearly equal. These matchups often bring out the miracle of courage and it makes me feel good to see such things, it lends me a bit of moxie.

To get through this game drinking helps a great deal, although I don't recommend it to many. Most drunks I've known aren't very interesting at all. Of course, most sober people aren't either.

On drugs, I've used them, of course, but laid off. Grass destroys motivation and always makes you late with no place to go. I can understand the heavier drugs with the exception of coke which takes you nowhere and doesn't even let you know you're there. What I mean by "understanding" the heavier drugs is that I can understand those who might choose that way: the fast bright trip and then out. Rather like an entertaining suicide, you know? But I'm an alky, you last longer, can type more . . . Meet more women, get into more jails . . .

About other things: yeh, I get fan mail, not too much, 7 or 8 letters a week, glad I'm not Burt Reynolds, and I can't answer them all but at times I do, especially if those letters are from a madhouse or a prison, or like one time from a madam of a house of prostitution and her girls. I can't help liking it that these people have read my work. I allow myself to feel good about that for a moment. I get many letters from people who say about the same thing: "If *you've* made it maybe there's a chance for me." In other words, they know I've been fucked around pretty badly but I'm still here. I don't mind them getting onto that as long as they don't beat on my door and come in and babble their troubles to me over a batch of 6-packs. I'm not here to save the People, I'm here to save my own coward's ass. And typing words down while I'm drinking seems to keep me on the roll. o.k.?

I'm not all that isolated. I've had my crutches: F. Dos, Turgenev, some of Celine, some of Hamsun, most of John Fante, a great deal of Sherwood Anderson, very early Hemingway, all of Carson McCullers, the longer poems of Jeffers; Nietzsche and Schopenhauer; the style of Saroyan without the content; Mozart, Mahler, Bach, Wagner, Eric Coates; Mondrian; e. e. cummings and the whores of east Hollywood; Jack Nicholson; Jackie Gleason; Charlie Chaplin, early; Baron Manfred von Richthofen; Leslie Howard; Bette Davis; Max Schmeling; Hitler . . . D. H. Lawrence, A. Huxley and the old bartender with the cadmium red face in Philly . . . And there was a particular actress whose name I can no longer think of, who I consider to be, has been the most beautiful woman of our times. She drank herself to death . . .

I get romantic, sure. I knew this gal once, she looked pretty fine. Used to be a girlfriend of E. Pound's. He mentions her in certain stanzas of the *Cantos*. Well, she went to see Jeffers one time. She knocked on his door. Maybe she wanted to be the only woman on earth who fucked both Pound and Jeffers. Well, Jeffers didn't answer his door. An old gal did. An aunt, a housekeeper, something, she didn't flash credentials. This beautiful gal told the old gal, "I want to see the master." "Wait a moment," said the old gal. Some time went by and then the old gal came by, came on out and said, "Jeffers said he's built his rock, go build yours . . ." I liked that story because I was having a lot of trouble with beautiful women at that time. But now I get to thinking, maybe the old gal never talked to

Jeffers at all, she just stood around, then came back and flashed the conversation upon the beauty. Well, I didn't get her either and I still haven't built my rock, although sometimes it's there when nothing else is around.

What I'm trying to say here is that nobody is ever famous or good, that's yesterday. Maybe you can get famous and good after you're dead but while you're alive, if anything counts, then if you can show some magic through the turmoil, it must be today's or tomorrow's, what you *have* done doesn't count for a shitsack full of cut-off rabbit's bungholes. This isn't a rule, it's a fact. And it's a fact when I get questions in the mail, I can't answer them. Or I'd be teaching a course in CREATIVE WRITING.

I realize I'm getting drunker but what could have been in a bad poem, you're getting here. I always remember reading the critical articles in the *Kenyon* [*Review*] and *Sewanee Review* in the old park bench days and I liked their use of language even though I thought it was fake, but all our words are fake finally, right, Bartender? What can we do? Not much. Get lucky maybe. We need the beat and a minor sense of entertainment before that moment they find us stiffened in the corner, useless, according to those left. I get terribly sad that we are so limited. But you're right, what is there to compare it to? That's no help. Let's drink up. And drink up again . . . trying to slice through all this shit with a small tin fork . . .

[To A. D. Winans]
February 23, 1983

[. . .] I was invited up to Naropa some time back, not for the [Jack] Kerouac [School of Disembodied Poetics] thing but for a 2 week stink, stint, I mean . . . First, I heard from some poetess [Anne Waldman] and I told her "no." Then I heard from Ginsberg and I had to tell him that I just don't do that sort of thing. The only thing I could tell most people about writing is, DON'T. It's all over-polluted now . . .

I never liked the beats, they were too self-promotional and the drugs gave them all wooden dicks or turned them into cunts. I'm from the old school, I believe in working and living in isolation; crowds weaken your intent and your originality . . . When you're hanging with writers you're not hearing or seeing anything but that. Or maybe my nature is just to grub it out alone. I feel good without anybody around.

—————

[To Jack Stevenson]
March 5, 1983

[. . .] Kafka, you're right . . . He's there. I always liked to read him when I was suicidal, he seemed to soothe me, his writing opened up this dark hole and you dropped right into it, he could show you little strange tricks, he took you a little bit off the streets. I had good luck with D. H. Lawrence this way too, when I was feeling shitty I dropped into his lurky twisting stuff and it was like leaving the god damned county, maybe even the country. Hemingway always makes you feel cheated like you've been tricked and worked over. Sherwood Anderson was an odd fuck and I liked to get lost in his sleepy and strange wanderings too. Well . . .

The poem with the misspelled word Bukowski talks about is "waiting for christmas," published in Blow *in 1983.*

[To John Martin]
October 3, 1983

10-3-83

Hello John:

enclosed new poems....

Also, mimeo poetry booklet with some of my poems and a nice review of HAM ON RYE. The thing is, in case I mailed you these poems, see first page in mag. 4th word first line should read "trugs". There isn't such a word as "turgs". For the record.

I hope HOT WATER MUSIC arrives soon. I get the idea that printer's and binders tend to set their own pace. Probably akin to trying to get a roofer to come by and fix a leaky roof.

all right,
your boy,

P.S.— I will be jumping between the novel, the short story and the poem, and I don't know why more don't do this. It's like having 3 women — when one goes sour you try one of the others. (HI, BABY!)

HE GOT A HAREM!

173

enclosed new poems. . . .

Also, mimeo poetry booklet with some of my poems and a nice review of *Ham on Rye*. The thing is, in case I mailed you these poems, see first page in mag. 4th word first line should read "trugs." There isn't such a word as "turgs." For the record.

I hope *Hot Water Music* arrives soon. I get the idea that printers and binders tend to set their own pace. Probably akin to trying to get a roofer to come by and fix a leaky roof.

P.S.—I will be jumping between the novel, the short story and the poem, and I don't know why more don't do this. It's like having 3 women—when one goes sour you try one of the others.

1984

[To William Packard]
May 19, 1984

Well, since you asked . . . otherwise, talking about poetry or the lack of it is just so much "sour grapes," a fruity expression of distaste used in the old days. Which is a rather crappy opening sentence, but I've only had one sip of wine. Old F. N[ietzsche] had it right when they asked him (also in the old days) about the poets. "The poets?" he said. "The poets lie too much." This was *one* of their faults, and if we are to find out what's wrong with or not right with modern poetry we'll have to look at the past also. You know that when the boys in the schoolyard don't want to read poetry, even laugh at it, look down at it as a sissified sport they aren't entirely wrong. Of course there is a change in semantics through time that makes absorbing past works more difficult but that isn't what put the boys off. Poetry just wasn't right, it was fake, it didn't matter. Take Shakespeare: reading him would dull you out of your mind. He only came up with it now and then, he'd give you a bright shot then go back to laboring up to the next point. The poets they fed us were immortal but they were neither dangerous or interesting. We spit them out and went about a more serious business: after school bloody-nose fights. Anybody knows that if you can't get into the young mind early it's going to be all hell getting into it late. People who turn out patriots and God-believers are very aware of this.

Poetry never had much going and it still doesn't. Yes, yes, I know, there was Li Po and some of the early Chinese poets who could compact great emotion and great truth into a few simple lines. There are other exceptions, of course, the human race is not so lame as to have not taken a few steps. But the vast bulk, pulp, ink and link of it all is treacherously empty, almost as if somebody had played a dirty trick on us, worse than that, and the libraries are a farce.

And the moderns borrow from the past and extend the error. Some claim that poetry is not for the many but for the few. So are most world governments. So are riches and the so-called class ladies. So are specially built toilets.

The best study of poetry is to read it and forget it. Because a poem can't be understood I don't think is a special virtue. Because most poets write from protected lives what they write about is limited. I'd much rather talk to a garbage man, a plumber or a fry cook than to a poet. They just know more about the common problems and the common joys of staying alive.

Poetry *can* be entertaining, it can be written with an astonishing clarity, I don't know why it has to be the other way, but it is. Poetry is like sitting in a stuffy room with the windows down. And very little is occurring to let in any air, any light. It could be that the field has simply drawn the worst of the practitioners. It seems so easy to call yourself "a poet." There's very little to do once you've assumed your stance. There's a reason why many people don't read poetry. The reason is that the stuff is badly and limply done. Perhaps the energetic creators have gone into music or prose or painting, sculpting? At least once in a while in these fields somebody breaks through the stale walls.

I stay away from the poets. When I was in my slum rooms it was more difficult to do this. When they found me they sat about gossiping and drinking my booze. Some of these poets were fairly well known. But their rancor, their bitching, and their envy of any other poet having any luck was unbelievable. Here were men who were supposed to be putting down words of verve and wisdom and exploration and they were just sick assholes, they couldn't even drink well, spittle drooled out of the edges of their mouths, they slobbered on their shirts, got giddy on a few drinks, puked and ranted. They bad-mouthed about everybody who wasn't around and there was little doubt in my mind that my turn would come when they were elsewhere. I didn't feel threatened. What mattered was after they left: their cheap vibes had settled under the rug and upon the window shades and all about and it was sometimes a day or two later until I felt all right again—I mean, my oh my:

"He's an Italian Jew cocksucker and his wife is in a madhouse."

"X is so cheap that when he goes downhill in his car he shuts off the motor and puts it in neutral."

"Y pulled down his pants and begged me to fuck him in the ass and asked me never to tell anybody."

"If I were a black homosexual I'd be famous. This way I don't stand a chance."

"Let's start a magazine. You got any money?"

Then there's the reading circuit. If you're doing it for the rent, all right. But too many do it for vanity. They'd read for free and many do. If I had wanted to be on stage I would have been an actor. To some who've come by and sucked up my drinks I've expressed my dislike for reading poems to an audience. It reeks of self-love, I've told them. I've seen these dandies get up and lisp their limpid verse, it's all so dull and tedious, and the audience too seems as flat as the reader: just dead people killing a dead night.

"Oh no, Bukowski, you're *wrong*! The troubadours used to go down the streets regaling the public!"

"Isn't it possible that they were bad?"

"Hey, *man,* what are you talking *about*? Madrigals! Songs of the heart! The poet is the same! We can't get *enough* poets! We need *more* poets, in the streets, on the mountaintops, everywhere!"

I suppose there are rewards for all this. After one of my readings down south, at a party afterwards, at the prof's house who had set up the reading, I was standing about drinking somebody else's booze for a change when the prof came up.

"Well, Bukowski, which one do you want?"

"You mean, of the women?"

"Yes, southern hospitality, you know."

There must have been between 15 and 20 women in the room. I glanced about and feeling it would save my god damned soul just a bit I selected an old one in a short red dress showing lots of leg, she was smeared with lipstick and booze.

"I'll take Grandma Moses there," I told him.

"What? No shit? Well, she's yours . . ."

I don't know how but word got around. Grandma was talking to some guy. She looked over and smiled, gave a little wave. I smiled, winked. I'd wrap that red dress around my balls.

Then the tall blonde came up. She had ivory face, the moulded features, the dark green eyes, the flanks, the mystery, the youth, ah, all that, you know, and she walked up and puffed out her enormous breasts and said, "You mean, you're going to take *that*?"

"Oh yes, mam, I'm going to carve my initials into one of her buns."

"YOU FOOL!" she spit at me and whirled off to talk to a young dark haired student with a delicate thin neck which bent forward wearily from his imagined agony. She was probably the leading poet-fucker of that town or maybe only the leading poet-sucker but I had spoiled her night. It does sometimes pay to read, even for 500 and air . . .

Which leads further. During this time with my little travel bag and my ever-widening sheath of poesy I met others of my ilk. Sometimes they were leaving as I was arriving or the other way around.

My god, they looked just as seedy, wild-eyed and depressed as I. Which gave me some hope for them. We're just hacking it, I thought, it's a dirty job and we know it. A few of these were writing some poetry that gambled a bit, screamed, seemed to be working toward something. I felt that we were hustling our shit against the odds, trying to stay out of the factories and the car washes, maybe even the madhouses. I know that just before my luck changed a little I was planning on trying to hold up some banks. Better to get fucked by an old woman in a short red dress . . . What I'm getting at, though, is that some of these few who began so well . . . say, almost with the same splash as an early Shapiro in *V-Letter,* now I looked around and they've been ingested, digested, suggested, molested, conquested, quiddled. They teach, they are poets-in-residence. They wear nice clothing. They are calm. But their writing is 4 flat tires and no spare in the trunk and no gas in the tank. NOW THEY TEACH POETRY. THEY TEACH HOW TO WRITE POETRY. Where did they get the idea that they ever knew anything about it? This is the mystery to me. How did they get so wise so fast and so dumb so fast? Where did they go? And why? And what for? Endurance is more important than truth because without endurance there can't be any truth. And truth means going to the end like you mean it. That way, death itself comes up short when it grabs.

Well, I've already said too much. I sound like those poets who used to come around and puke on my couch. And my word is just another word in with all the others' words. Just to let you know I've got a new kitten. Male. I need a name. For the kitten, I mean. And there have been some good names. Don't you think? Like Jeffers. E. E. Cummings. Auden. Stephen Spender. Catullus. Li Po. Villon. Neruda. Blake. Conrad Aiken. And there's Ezra. Lorca. Millay. I don't know.

Ah, hell, maybe I'll just name the son of a bitch "Baby Face Nelson" and be done with it.

[To A. D. Winans]
June 27, 1984

[. . .] I think one of the best things that ever happened to me was that I was so long unsuccessful as a writer and had to work for a living until I was 50. It kept me away from other writers and their parlor games and their backbiting and their bitching, and now that I've had some luck I still intend to absent myself from them.

Let them continue their attacks, I will continue my work, which is not something I do to seek immortality or even a minor fame. I do it because I must and I will. I feel good most of the time, especially when I'm at this machine, and the words feel more and more as if they are coming out better and better. True or not, right or wrong, I go with it.

[To Carl Weissner]
August 2, 1984

[. . .] The work you've done over the years for me and the Sparrow, your translations and your efforts to always get the best for us has to be one of the most remarkable things I know of. Two of the luckiest things that ever happened to me were when Martin picked me up and you decided to be my translator and agent, and friend. Then too, I think of old Jon Webb who published me in those splendid editions when I was virtually unknown. There are magic people in the world, and you are most surely one of them. [. . .]

Here, well, I get so many books of translation from so many places I hardly know what's going on. The book case can't hold them all. They are all over the rug. Need another bookcase in the bedroom. Maybe soon. It's all very strange. To think that people in all these far away countries are sitting about reading *Women, Factotum, South of No North, Ham on Rye* and on and on . . . I get love letters from ladies in far off places. A lady in Australia sent me the key to her house. Long letters from others. And here, in the U.S., I get offers from girls from 19 to 21 to come see me. I tell them, nothing doing. Nothing is free. There is a price on everything. I tell them to go fuck somebody their own age. [. . .]

Martin has me on the paintings for *War All the Time*. I try to tell him that the paintings come from the same place the writing comes from and that I'd rather write. I can't make him see this. So I sit about drunk squeezing paint tubes onto paper and placing them on the floor and the cats walk over them. I don't stop them.

1985

The book removed from the Nijmegen library, in the Netherlands, was Erections, Ejaculations, Exhibitions and General Tales of Ordinary Madness.

[To Hans van den Broek]
January 22, 1985

Thank you for your letter telling me of the removal of one of my books from the Nijmegen library. And that it is accused of discrimination because of the black people, homosexuals and women. And that it is sadism because of the sadism.

The thing that I fear discriminating against is humor and truth.

If I write badly about blacks, homosexuals and women it is because those who I met were that. There are many "bads"—bad dogs, bad censorship; there are even "bad" white males. Only when you write about "bad" white males they don't complain about it. And need I say that there are "good" blacks, "good" homosexuals and "good" women?

In my work, as a writer, I only photograph, in words, what I see. If I write of "sadism" it is because it exists. I didn't invent it, and if some terrible act occurs in my work it is because such things happen in our lives, I am not on the side of evil, if such a thing as evil abounds. In my writing I do not always agree with what occurs, nor do I linger in the mud for the sheer sake of it. Also, it is curious that people who rail against my work seem to overlook the sections of it which entail joy and love and hope, and there are such sections. My days, my years, my life have seen ups and downs, lights and darknesses. If I wrote only and continually of the "light" and never mentioned the other, then as an artist I would be a liar.

Censorship is the tool of those who have the need to hide actualities from themselves and from others. Their fear is only their inability to face what is real, and I can't vent any anger against them, I only feel this appalling sadness. Somewhere, in their upbringing, they were shielded against the total facts of our existence. They were only taught to look one way when many ways exist.

I am not dismayed that one of my books has been hunted down and is dislodged from the shelves of a local library. In a sense, I am honored that I have written something that has awakened these from their non-ponderous depths. But I am hurt, yes, when somebody else's book is censored, for that book usually is a great book and there are few of those, and throughout the ages that type of book has often generated into a classic, and what was once thought shocking and immoral is now required reading at many of our universities.

I am not saying that my book is one of those, but I am saying that in our time, at this moment when any moment may be the last for most of us, it's damned galling and impossibly sad that we still have among us the small, bitter people, the witch-hunters and the declaimers against reality. Yet, these too belong with us, they are part of the whole, and if I haven't written about them, I should, maybe have here, and that's enough.

may we all get better together.

[To A. D. Winans]
February 22, 1985

[. . .] On quitting your job at 50, I don't know what to say. I had to quit mine. My whole body was in pain, could no longer lift my arms. If somebody touched me, just that touch would send reams and shots of agony through me. I was finished. They had beat on my body and mind for decades. And I didn't have a dime. I had to drink it away to free my mind from what was occurring. I decided that I would be better off on skid row. I mean that. It had come to a faltering end. My last day on the job, some guy let a remark fall as I walked by: "That old guy has a lot of guts to quit a job at *his* age." I didn't feel I had an age. The years had just added up and shitted away.

Yeah, I had fear. I had fear I could never make it as a writer, moneywise. Rent, child support. Food didn't matter. I just drank and sat at the machine. Wrote my first novel (*Post Office*) in 19 nights. I drank beer and scotch and sat around in my shorts. I smoked cheap cigars and listened to the radio. I wrote dirty stories for the sex mags. It got the rent and also got the soft ones and the safe ones to say: He hates women. My income tax returns for those first years show ridiculously little money earned but somehow I was existing. The poetry readings came and I hated them but it was more $$$. It was a drunken wild fog of a time and I had some luck. And I wrote and wrote and wrote, I loved the banging of the typer. I was fighting for each day. And I lucked it with a good landlord and landlady. They thought I was crazy. I went down and drank with them every other night. They had a refrig. stacked with nothing but quart bottles of Eastside Beer. We drank out of the quarts, one after the other until 4 a.m., singing songs of the 20's and 30's.

"You're crazy," my landlady kept saying, "you quit that good job in the post office." "And now you're going with that crazy woman. You know she's crazy, don't you?" the landlord would say.

Also, I got ten bucks a week for writing that column "Notes of a Dirty Old Man." And I mean, that ten bucks looked big sometimes.

I don't know, A. D., I don't quite know how I made it. The drinking always helped. It still does. And, frankly, I loved to write! THE SOUND OF THE TYPER. Sometimes I think it was only the sound of the typer that I wanted. And the drink there, beer with scotch, by the side of the machine. And finding cigar stubs, old ones, lighting them while drunk and burning my nose. It wasn't so much that I was TRYING to be a writer, it was more like doing something that felt good to do.

The luck gradually mounted and I kept writing. The women got younger and more demanding. And certain writers began to hate me. They still do, only more so. That doesn't matter. What matters is that I didn't die on that post office stool. Security? Security to what?

[To John Martin]
June 1985

You've made a living at it, and mostly have published what you've wanted to, perhaps not so much at the beginning when you tended to listen more to "literary" voices who wanted to point you toward "prestige," but more and more you've become the gambler, one who gambles but still tends to win—out of style and knowledge, instinct. What sells is not necessarily good and what doesn't sell can really be bad, rather than a misunderstood Art-form. There are all manners of this admixture. Running a good show takes an Eye which can separate the bull from the bullshit. You do your work with an energy which boggles the slack, lackadaisical wishes and dreams of those who think things might arrive without the good fight.

They talk you down for making things work when they can't make things work; their envy is wrought out of their pitiful weakness. You simply go ahead, continue, while they rail at their seeming misfortune which is only brought about by a gross laziness and a licorice stick-like backbone.

You are the publisher, the editor, the script reader, the bill-collector, the publicist, and Christ knows what else, while you listen to the so-called Great Ones moaning and groaning over the telephone about all manners of trivial animosities, the tender two-bit troubles that trouble every living creature but which *they* feel particularly set-upon because of their very sensitive and chosen, so-called, God-given tenfold genius.

You do your fucking work and you do it well, very well, but what bothers me, even if it doesn't bother you, is what I consider your almost lack of recognition for what you do, have done, continue to do, relentlessly and with force. I dare say you've published a body of literature for almost three decades that stands unsurpassed in the history of publishing in America. Yet, what is said about you? Not that you need it, only that I need it for you. I prefer Champions not to go unnoticed.

Your problem is that in doing your work you have forsaken the time to go to all the cocktail parties and to kiss the asses of the media and university creatures who would boost you into the circle of their dull and death-like prominence.

Don't worry, the Bomb will be soon enough and if not, the record of your accomplishments will be there, Black Sparrow, you foolish wonderful kind son of a bitch.

The books Bukowski discusses below are The Road to Los Angeles *and* The Wine of Youth, *both published posthumously by Black Sparrow Press in 1985.*

[To Joyce Fante]
December 18, 1985

I'm sorry you asked about John's book and I have sat about for days and some nights wondering how to answer you and there's no way I can do it but this way: I didn't like it or the book which followed.

You know, there is a way of having rancor with style, and there is a way of indulging bitterness with humor but both of these books just made me feel very bad. It's all right to ravage if your ravage takes courage but if it's just ravage for the sake of ravage, well, that's done every day in all of our lives, it happens on the freeways and alleys of our goings and comings and waitings.

John was my main influence, along with Celine and Dostoevsky and Sherwood Anderson, and he wrote some of the most feeling and grace-filled books of our time but I feel that these latter or earlier works would have been better left unpublished. I could be wrong, of course. I am often wrong.

That I was able to meet my hero (if you'll pardon that term) late in his life and under the most painful conditions, was both a very sad and a very great thing for me. And I hope that the few words that I had with John helped him in the middle of that most terrible hell.

For it all, I will always remember reading *Ask the Dust,* which I still consider the finest novel written in all time, a novel which probably saved my life, for whatever it is worth.

Nobody is ever on top of their game at all times; in fact, few ever get very close. John did, and more than once. You lived with a very bitter man who overcame his bitterness, finally, with a love that rang and filled and jostled each line into a memorable miracle that said

> yes in spite of no
> yes because of no
> which said
> yes yes yes

and continued to say it, even as I met him as he was.

There will never be another John Fante . . .

He was a bulldog with heart, in hell.

1986

[To Kurt Nimmo]
March 3, 1986

I'm sorry Martin is looming over you in nightmare propor-
tions. I'm the ace in his stable and it fidgets him into near madness
to have anybody leak out with a few scattered poems. [*Relentless as
the*] *Tarantula* was beautifully done and I think the poems are o.k.,
a couple of them even really exceptional. Frankly, I am happy that
you did it . . .

Martin has thousands of my poems, thousands, thousands, a
build-up of 20 years of sending him work. He could run off 5 or 6 or
7 books of my poetry without any problem and the poems would all
be of high level. I just write an awful lot of stuff.

Martin is deliberately holding off on my next book to make
them eager and hungry. He talks about the way Col. Parker handled
E. Presley. He said he held the Presley stuff back to make them
want him. Shit, all those dumb Presley movies. I don't call that
holding back.

Martin and I more or less started together and I feel that I
owe him some loyalty; on the other hand, he might not even be in
the game now if it weren't for me.

I just hate to get into these scratching games . . . with Martin.
All I want to do is drink wine and type.

He sent me a copy of the letter he wrote to you. Then why the phone call? To you . . .

Martin seems over-obsessed with the whole fucking thing.

From my viewpoint it appears to me that you simply published the poems because you liked them. And then you *give* the copies away to your subscribers . . . Doesn't sound to me like you're trying to destroy Martin's empire!

[To John Martin]
March 5, 1986

This stuff is hell.

What I am beginning to realize is that Black Sparrow can only publish what it wants to.

What is left over you still have in your backlogs.

It's like you have a freak monkey in a cage to display at your behest.

My energy is being mutilated for your simple profit motive.

You keep holding back on me while my readers are in a rage for a taste of more.

My loyalty to you began as a fair and even matter.

All I want to do is to type this shit. And you only allow the people to see maybe one-sixth of my energy.

This is murder. You are killing me.

No poet in his time has been restricted as you are restricting me.

[To William Packard]
March 27, 1986

Just got *NYQ* #29 and noted the many Chinaski poems you published! You make a man feel like e. e. Cummings or almost maybe a bit like Ezra, and Li Po and I suck at this wine tonight and feel excellently good; I like to make the words bite into the paper not so much like Hemingway did but more like scratches in ice and also attended with some small laughter.

Thank you for your gamble. I am sure that in many quarters I am considered "unpoetic," which, of course, pleases me to the timbers.

So, ah . . . umm . . . I . . . enclose some more, even though I realize you are even now overloaded. If the *NYQ* hadn't arrived I woulda shot for somewhere else but I got into this high elation and sent them toward you. This is no sell-job . . . If all returns, there is just so much space for so many people, and I will move these toward somewhere . . .

It took me some decades to get lucky and I think that was best—the crappy jobs, the bad-ass women, meanwhile reading the writers and getting very little out of them. When you are a slave and a servant to somebody else's dollar there is something about most writing that fails to please. Of course, youth has something about it that makes you think you are much better than you are. Early on, I wrote too much like Saroyan and Hemingway and a little bit like Sherwood Anderson. Then I began to dislike Saroyan because he failed to alter to conditions and Hemingway because there was no fucking humor, so those dried out of me. Sherwood Anderson, well a lot of him still sticks. Li Po woulda liked him.

Anyhow, as I failed at the machine I went more and more to drink and women, it was like writing in a substitute fashion and it damned near killed me but I was ready to be killed and it didn't quite happen, and even though I quit the other kind of writing, I was unwittingly gathering some strange and wild material which maybe somebody chasing a Doctorate in Literature at some Univ. wouldn't fall upon. You know, I've had well-meaning people tell me: "Everybody suffers." I always tell them, "Nobody suffers like the poor." Then I get rid of them.

Writing is only the result of what we have become day by day over the years. It's a god damned fingerprint of self and there it is. And all that was written in the past is nothing; what it is . . . is only the next line. And when you can't come up with the next line it doesn't mean you're old, it means you're dead. It's all right to be dead, it happens. I yearn for a postponement, though, as do all of us. One more sheet of paper into this machine, under this hot desk lamp, stuck within the wine, re-lighting these cigarette stubs as downstairs my poor wife hears these sounds, wondering if I'm mad or just drunk or whatever. I never show her my work, I never talk about it. When the luck holds and a book comes out, I go to bed, read it, say nothing, pass it to her. She reads it, says very little. This is the way the gods will have it. This is a life beyond all mortal and moral considerations. This is it. Fixed like this. And when my skeleton rests upon the bottom of the casket, should I have that, nothing will be able to subtract from these splendid nights, sitting here at this machine.

[To Carl Weissner]
August 22, 1986

[. . .] I've gulped down damn near a full bottle in 15 minutes, chilled white. Have to, it gets warm so fast. Rather like the new book, *You Get So Alone at Times That It Just Makes Sense.* Nothing immortal but some good laughs, maybe? When Barbet was over he saw all these cardboard boxes full of poems.

"Jesus Christ, did you write all this stuff?" he asked.

"This year," I said.

"Does Martin select your best stuff?"

"Let's hope so . . ."

Well, most poets select their own poems. Me, I'm lazy. Also, while I am working at selecting poems I could be writing *more*. One of Martin's great secrets is that he has these THOUSANDS OF POEMS UNDER COVER. He'll never print them all, he won't live that long. I'm probably a touch mad, but hardly ever feel I write when I don't feel like writing. As per Martin, I only wish he would print the wilder poems. I sense he's making me a touch too formal.

I gotta get back to writing the fucking short story. It's a great form, you can play around more. It's just that, I can write a story when I'm feeling good and I haven't been feeling fucking good at all, hence all the poems poems poems . . . Without that release I would probably be a suicide or popping pills at the nearest mental institute.

1988

[To Carl Weissner]
July 6, 1988

[. . .] The poems get in the way of the novel—others besides skin cancer wails—keep coming. Sometimes only the bottle and the poem will fit a situation, or a week of situations. Or weeks of.

Still up to page 173 on novel [*Hollywood*], pages no longer grip on clipboard. I think the writing is all right, although if and when the book comes out I may have further troubles. But our law courts are so stuffed here that sometimes before a case comes up it's 5 or 6 years, during which counter papers fly about and papers and the lawyers get fat and rich while the clients go mad.

Gargoyle, yes, they have been around a long time although the work they print seems rather smooth and lacking in gamble and nerve. Jay D[ougherty] tells me, though, that you have come up with a roaring interview and I look forward to what Kool Karl from Mannheim comes forth with. I've always liked your angles on existence.

Roominghouse [*Madrigals*], yes, but I still like what I am doing now. A clarity closer to the bone. I think. As long as I've been fucking with the ribbon I ought to have a touch with this thing.

194

[To Carl Weissner]
November 6, 1988

[. . .] Yes, I finished *Hollywood*. I think it is all right. Some bellylaughs within. Actually, I like it as well as anything I have written. But a writer, of course, is the worst judge of his own work. But writing it was a tonic for me, an elixir, yah, because a lot of things were eating at me, gnawing at me, yelling at me and the typewriter and the page was a way out, clean out of the shitpond into a rather airy half-light even though what I was writing about was a horror story. Sometimes everything seems to fit when there seems no chance.

I'd much rather prefer to write from a happy state of mind and can do so when that rare and lucky bit arrives. I don't believe in pain as a pusher of art. Pain is too often. We can breathe without it. If it will let us.

On Burroughs, I never had much luck with him. And I'm sorry that he has dimmed for you. That whole gang: Ginsberg, Corso, Burroughs, so forth, they long ago dimmed for me. When you write only to get famous you shit it away. I don't want to make rules but if there is one it is: the only writers who write well are those who must write in order not to go mad.

1990

Hughes published four Bukowski poems in the Sycamore Review *in 1990-91.*

[To Henry Hughes]
September 13, 1990

9-13-90

Hello Henry Hughes:

I'm glad I got a couple past you.

I'm 70 now but as long as the red wine flows and the typewriter goes, it's all right. It was a good show for me when I was writing dirty stories for the men's mags to get the rent and it's still a good show for me as I write against the hazards of a little fame and a little money--and those approaching footsteps on that thing with the STOP sign. At times I've enjoyed this contest with life. On the other hand, I'll leave it without regrets.

Sometimes I've called writing a disease. If so, I'm glad that it caught me. I've never walked into this room and looked at this typewriter without feeling that something somewhere, some strange gods or something utterly unnamable has touched me with a blithering, blathering and wonderous luck that holds and holds and holds. Oh yes.

196

I'm glad I got a couple past you.

I'm 70 now but as long as the red wine flows and the typewriter goes, it's all right. It was a good show for me when I was writing dirty stories for the men's mags to get the rent and it's still a good show for me as I write against the hazards of a little fame and a little money—and those approaching footsteps on that thing with the STOP sign. At times I've enjoyed this contest with life. On the other hand, I'll leave it without regrets.

Sometimes I've called writing a disease. If so, I'm glad that it caught me. I've never walked into this room and looked at this typewriter without feeling that something somewhere, some strange gods or something utterly unnamable has touched me with a blithering, blathering and wondrous luck that holds and holds and holds. Oh yes.

———

[To the editors of the *Colorado North Review*]
September 15, 1990

[. . .] I note that you are university affiliated but that you still sound quite human, at least in your correspondence. But I have noted in the last couple of years that a few university publications are more open to gamble and divergence in what they promulgate, I mean they seem to be climbing out of the 19th century at least as the 21st approaches. A lovely sign indeed.

Yes, I know what you mean about writing and writers. We seem to have lost the target. Writers seem to write to be known as writers. They don't write because something is driving them toward the edge. I look back at when Pound, T. S. Eliot, e. e. Cummings, Jeffers, Auden, Spender were about. Their work cracked right through the paper, set it on fire. Poems became events, explosions. There was a high excitement. Now, for decades there has seemed to be this lull, almost a *practiced* lull, as if dullness indicated genius. And if a new talent came along it was only a flash, a few poems, a thin book and then he or she was sanded down, ingested into the quiet nothingness. Talent without durability is a god damned crime. It means they went to the soft trap, it means they believed the praise, it means they settled short. A writer is not a writer because he has written some books. A writer is not a writer because he teaches literature. A writer is only a writer if he can write now, tonight, this minute. We have too many x-writers who type. Books fall from my hand to the floor. They are total crap. I think we have just blown away half a century to the stinking winds.

Yes, the classical composers. I always write with the music on and a bottle of good red. And smoke Mangalore Ganesh beedies. The whirling of the smoke, the banging of the typer and the music. What a way to spit in the face of death and to congratulate it at the same time. Yes.

[To Kevin Ring]
September 16, 1990

[. . .] I know what you mean about poetry. The stale pretensiveness of it has bothered me for decades, not only the poetry of our time but the poetry of the ages, the so-called best stuff. It seems like everybody's preening, putting-on, burning on too low a flame or none at all, making it pretty, making it delicate [. . .] Prose comes pretty close behind. I am not inferring that I am a great writer but I am saying that as a reader I feel cheated, lardedover, pissed upon with obvious tricks of the trade, tricks hardly worth learning.

Oh yes, I know about Sir Edward Elgar. He could write for Queen and country and still trill the magic. There's also Eric Coates. I speak here of the English. There are so many great classical composers throughout time. I listen to hours of it, it's my drug. It smooths the kinks in my poor ravaged brain. Unlike the poets and prose writers, the classical composers seem quite honest, enduring and full of invention and fire. I can't get enough of them, the list seems endless. So many of them virtually laid down their lives for their work. The ultimate gamble. I listen to hours of classical music, get most of it from the radio, and even after so many years I often hear a new and striking work that has seldom been played.

Those are the great nights when I hear one of those works. I know the standards and the standard arrangements, but no matter how good, when you have somehow memorized each note about to arrive, it does take a little away. My writing, although simple in its way, is always guided by music because I listen as I write, and, of course, there's the dear old bottle.

———

[To William Packard]
December 23, 1990

[. . .] When everything works best it's not because you chose writing but because writing chose you. It's when you're mad with it, it's when it's stuffed in your ears, your nostrils, under your fingernails. It's when there's no hope but that.

Once in Atlanta, starving in a tar paper shack, freezing. There were only newspapers for a floor. And I found a pencil stub and I wrote on the white margins of the edges of those newspapers with the pencil stub, knowing that nobody would ever see it. It was a cancer madness. And it was never work or planned or part of a school. It was. That's all.

And why do we fail? It's the age, something about the age, our Age. For half a century there has been nothing. No real breakthrough, no newness, no blazing energy, no gamble.

What? Who? Lowell? That grasshopper? Don't sing me crap songs.

We do what we can and we don't do very well.

Strictured. Locked. We *pose* at it.

We work too hard. We try too hard.

Don't try. Don't work. It's there. It's looking right at us, aching to kick out of the closed womb.

There's been too much *direction*. It's all free, we needn't be told.

Classes? Classes are for asses.

Writing a poem is as easy as beating your meat or drinking a bottle of beer. Look. Here's one:

"flux"

mother saw the raccoon,
my wife told me.

ah, I said.

and that was
just about
the shape of things
tonight.

1991

[To John Martin]
March 11, 1991, 1:42 AM

I am probably writing too much. For me, it can't be. I'm hooked on it.

In the center of my brain I still remember that time in Atlanta, repeat it as I might, when I was starving and out of my mind, but maybe in my mind, when I wrote with a pencil stub on the white edges of the newspapers my landowners had placed upon that earthen floor as a rug. Mad? Sure, but good mad, I'd like to think. One doesn't forget, ever. I had the best university training in Literature anybody ever had. I'm out to blast through the ceiling of everywhere. Just to do it.

[To John Martin]
March 23, 1991, 11:36 PM

I keep getting this feeling that I am a beginning writer. The old excitement and wonder are there . . . It's a great madness. I think too many writers, after they have been in the game for some time, get too practiced, too careful. They are afraid to make mistakes. You roll the dice, you're going to get snake eyes, sometimes.

201

I like to keep it loose and wild. A good tight poem can happen but it comes along while you are working with something else. I know I write some crap but by letting it go, banging the drums, there's a juicy freedom in that.

I'm having myself a rife, ripe, rapacious, ripping time. So far, the gods are allowing me this celebration. It's so strange. But I'll take it.

[To John Martin]
April 13, 1991, 12:20 AM

Bought this green paper by mistake but it works pretty good, I think.

Just signed a couple of books for Fidel Castro. I have no politics, of course, but it's time he read some Black Sparrow, what?

[To Patrick Foy]
April 15, 1991, 8:34 PM

Thanks for poem and photo, both good. No, I'm not a tennis freak but am a student of defeat. Have had a few lessons there.

Have meant to tell you about the good reads you've sent along. Your fight against the inbred stupidity of the history of this century is a noble and a lonely one. I marvel at how you persist against the odds. I believe that your views are on the mark. But the past propaganda has sunk almost all minds into an oblivious acceptance of the deathly lie. They are unable to go back and undo the massive errors because then our vaunted leaders, our historical heroes would be uncovered as frauds and fakes. And think of the millions of lives lost for so-called great causes. All these lives, then, would have to be admitted as totally wasted, not for the right reasons but for all the wrong ones. This monstrous game is too far gone to be righted; it would drive men and mothers, almost everybody, to rage and madness. But what is the most horrifying thing of all is that the game continues, not only in the same fashion but in a more soulless way through the same greed and fear, and through a practice learned and honed so well that the bigger the liars, the more they will be believed in.

All those few of us who are aware can do is to protect our own minds against this onslaught which has erased the sensibilities of almost all humans.

[To John Martin]
July 12, 1991, 9:39 PM

Read where Henry Miller stopped writing after he became famous. Which probably meant he wrote to become famous. I don't understand this: there is nothing more magic and beautiful than lines forming across paper. It's all there is. It's all there ever was. No reward is greater than the doing. What comes afterwards is more than secondary. I can't understand any writer who stops writing. It's like taking your heart out and flushing it away with the turds. I'll write to my last god damned breath, whether anybody thinks it's good or not. The end as the beginning. I was meant to be like this. It's as simple and profound as that. Now let me stop writing about this so that I can write about something else.

1992

[To John Martin]
January 19, 1992, 12:16 AM

Short journal entry enclosed.

Thanks for the rundown on sales. Truly amazing. That you keep these 18 books in print and that they keep selling. It's strange to me and I'm proud of each book, the fact that they are still kicking and alive. And there's something about the old titles, as time goes on they seem to take on an extra flavor (I mean, the actual book titles) as if they had a way of their own. Well, it's great, one of those quiet miracles.

And best, we're still at it. You ever lay it down and I don't know what I will do. We've worked in total trust and harmony, I don't ever remember a single argument about anything.

Thanks, old boy, it's been beautiful.

[To William Packard]
March 30, 1992, 8:24 PM

[. . .] Thanks for the enclosures. I like your poem "The Seducer." You know how it works. Or doesn't work. Thanks too for enclosing the syllabus. I am honored to be on the same card as Pound, Lorca, Williams and Auden. *Mockingbird Wish Me Luck*. And speaking of Pound, many decades ago I was shacked with a lady and I was a poor provider and how we made it, drinking continually as we did, I am truly amazed at now, although then I didn't think much about it. Anyhow, in the few non-drinking moments I usually made my way to the library and back. One time I opened the door and stood there with that heavy book in my hand and she looked up from the bed and said, "You got them god damned *Cantos* again?" "Yes," I told her, "we can't fuck *all* the time."

Jack Grapes, editor of the literary magazine Onthebus, *published a large number of poems and journal entries by Bukowski in a section called "A Charles Bukowski Album." Grapes also reviewed Bukowski's poetry.*

[To Jack Grapes]
October 22, 1992, 12:10 PM

Thanks for the good letter and for letting me see your piece on *It Catches*. Also, for letting me know about the album. 32 pages, that's some run.

You know, *It Catches* was that time and it was a strange time and I wasn't even young then. And now, there's 72 years riding me, and it's much like trying to overcome the factory or a bad shack job. I feel that the writing is still there, I can feel the words biting into the paper, it's as needed as ever [. . .] Writing has saved me from the madhouse, from murder and suicide. I still need it. Now. Tomorrow. Until the last breath.

The hangovers are worse for me now but I still get out of bed, into the car and out to the track. I make my plays. The other bettors never bother me. "That guy doesn't talk to anybody."

Then at night, sometimes it's there on the computer. If it isn't, I don't shove it through. Unless the words jump out of you, forget it. Sometimes I don't get near the computer because nothing's buzzing and I'm either dead or resting and only time will tell. But I'm dead until the next line appears on the screen. It's not a holy thing but it's wholly necessary. Yeah. Yes. Meanwhile, I try to be as human as possible: talk to my wife, pet my cats, sit and watch tv if I am able or maybe just read the newspaper from first page to last or maybe just sleep early. Being 72 is another adventure. When I'm 92 I'll look back at that and laugh. No, I've gone about far enough. It's too much like the same movie. Except for all of us it's getting a little uglier. I never thought I'd be here now and when I go, I'll be ready.

1993

After unsuccessfully trying to appear in Poetry *magazine for over four decades, Bukowski finally had three poems published shortly before his passing away.*

[To Joseph Parisi]
February 1, 1993, 10:31 PM

I remember, as a very young man, sitting around the L.A. public library reading *Poetry: A Magazine of Verse.* Now, at last, I have joined you. I suppose it was a matter left up to the both of us. Anyhow, I'm glad I got a couple of poems past you. [. . .]

Thank you, the new year is treating me kindly. What I mean is, the words are forming and churning, spinning and flying for me. The older I get, the more this magic madness seems to fall upon me. Very odd, but I'll accept it.

Afterword

While going over some two thousand pages of unpublished correspondence in an effort to find Bukowski's most insightful letters on writing, I came across all kinds of never-before-seen gems: obscure letters to Henry Miller, Whit Burnett, Caresse Crosby, Lawrence Ferlinghetti, and his literary god, John Fante; a forgotten, colorful blurb for one of Bukowski's most popular books, *Erections, Ejaculations, Exhibitions and General Tales of Ordinary Madness;* an introduction that Bukowski wrote for his first book in Dutch, *Dronken Mirakels & Andere Offers,* first published in English here; and an unfinished parody of literary magazines, titled *The Paper Toilet Review.* There were also a few early letters where Bukowski's tone is strikingly ornate and contrived, as well as some breathtaking illustrations made public here for the first time ever. Add to this rare material some of the most passionate letters Bukowski ever wrote, and this volume of correspondence is easily as compelling as any other of his collections. Indeed, it's Bukowski at his best: raw, witty, and deeply moving, taking no prisoners while delivering the goods.

For the most part, these letters have a distinct sense of immediacy; having little time for shop talk, Bukowski pours himself forth in every single letter, discussing daily events with genuine excitement. It is as if Bukowski were writing poems in letter form—he repeatedly claims that letters are as important as poems. Similarly, some of the letters read like stories, as if he were actually writing a well-developed short story. Poetry, fiction, and correspondence fall into the very same category for Bukowski: art. He is equally intense when addressing people for the first time. His letters to Edward van Aelstyn and Jack Conroy are as truly Bukowskian as the letters he sent to friends, editors, and poets he had been corresponding with for extended periods of time. To Bukowski, there was no difference. Letters were a vehicle to express who he was, no matter to whom he was writing.

Spontaneity is also obvious in Bukowski's correspondence. First thought, best thought, he seems to say in most letters. His voice comes ringing through in its full first-person glory when writing to friends and enemies alike. Stripped of all pretense, his letter writing becomes a crystal-clear snapshot of Bukowski's mood at the time. His no-holds-barred approach to creation is definitely present in his correspondence, whether he is writing an impassioned statement about the lay of the land in American letters, with a tender aside about his daughter, or making a vicious attack on contemporary writers. Through it all, Bukowski remains the same.

There are some notable exceptions, though. In his letters to Whit Burnett, Caresse Crosby, Henry Miller, and John Fante, Bukowski sounds somewhat contrived, even sheepish, as if he didn't want to upset them. Similarly, in the letters from the late 1950s, his style is more elaborate, deliberately and mockingly cultish, invoking what he calls "dictionary words" for humorous effect. This same change appears in his poetry: the early poetry can be convoluted and ornate whereas the late poetry has "a clarity closer to the bone," as he said of the poems he was writing in the late 1980s. The tone of his correspondence shifts in this direction in the early 1960s, especially when he begins corresponding with Jon

Webb and William Corrington. Earlier trickeries are replaced by a straightforward prose. Bukowski at this point begins to sound like the "Bukowski" most readers are familiar with.

For both the early and the late Bukowski, writing was akin to a pleasant disease no one could cure, and these letters show how much Bukowski valued the joy of writing. It was a natural force he could not and did not want to stop, no matter what, like a rough river taking him into the unknown in stormy weather. Bukowski seldom experienced writer's block, and he wrote indefatigably almost daily over a period of fifty years. He graphically expressed his urge to write in a 1987 interview: "If I don't write for a week, I get sick. I can't walk, I get dizzy. I lay in bed, I puke. Get up in the morning and gag. I've got to type. If you chopped my hands off, I'd type with my feet." His prolific and disciplined nature reveal what really made him happy: "No reward is greater than the doing. What comes afterward is more than secondary," he confided in the early 1990s. Add to that a strong entertainment element Bukowski always championed in his work, and the outcome is as classic as you can get: writing as *dulce et utile*, as Horace suggested centuries ago.

Entrenched in his small Los Angeles apartments, Bukowski lived isolated from the outer world. He was so utterly unconcerned by current events that when he was accused of having missed the 1960s, he wryly replied: "Hell, yes, I was [working] in the post office." Like his idol Robinson Jeffers in Big Sur, Bukowski feverishly created in complete solitude; like Fyodor Dostoevsky's underground man, he fired off his incendiary projectiles from his anonymous den, leaving readers and publishers dumbfounded. In an almost desperate attempt to be out of touch with the Establishment, Bukowski sent out his ageless missiles against the uptight literary arena to stir it up. It is precisely that timelessness that makes his work everlasting and memorable.

German born, Bukowski grew up in Los Angeles in a family deprived of love and affection, which would shape his rock-hard and individualistic, almost Nietzschean, view of the world. Being a Depression kid, and older than most emerging writers, fashionable trends like the counterculture of the 1960s or the skin-deep Flower Power ideology attracted only his scorn. What Bukowski despised the most was the gregariousness and egotism of popular groups such as the Beats, who seemed to believe that being in the limelight was more important than doing the actual work. Bukowski secluded himself from that brouhaha to devote himself to writing. The typewriter took him to that hard-to-pinpoint place between sanity and madness that he loved so much. Writing was the only way he knew to keep madness at bay.

By nature a lone wolf, Bukowski liked to quote Sartre's line that "hell is other people," yet he never tried to deny his many literary influences. Alcohol and classical music were also obvious influences on his writing, probably as much as any of the artists he looked up to, whom he duly thanked in many of his letters. He was also grateful to some of his small-press editors, especially Jon Webb, Marvin Malone, and John Martin and their "magic journey" together. At the same time, he repeatedly put down most highly regarded writers, including Shakespeare and Faulkner. Contemporary authors were also not spared: Carol Bergé, Ron Silliman, Henry Miller (and his "Star Trek babbling"), and Robert Creeley were all viciously attacked—uncharacteristically, Bukowski changed his view on Creeley in the early 1970s, admitting his criticism was unfounded. As Bukowski said more than once, he began to write not because he was good but because the other writers were so bad.

Not a learned man by any standards, Bukowski did go to college for a year and a half, and he was proud of having read untold numbers of books at the Los Angeles Public Library as a young man. Although he consistently misspelled the name of many well-

known authors, this infamously crude drunk lecher could quote almost verbatim long-forgotten medieval lyrics, various aphorisms by Nietzsche, and many lines from poems by Shakespeare, Whitman, and other literary giants. So much for the ignorant Dirty Old Man of American letters.

Not only that, Bukowski could be fastidious about grammar. In the "leave us be fair" versus "let us be fair" dilemma in the April 2, 1959, letter to Anthony Linick, Bukowski comically delivers a blow against grammar rules. Furthermore, when the editors of literary magazines published his poems with the occasional typographical error, he became an angry old man spewing invectives right and left. For a prolific author who almost had no time for revision, Bukowski could be finicky—and rightly so—about typos, which were common in the mimeographed little magazines that published his work in record time.

Non-writing matters, such as submitting manuscripts to hundreds of literary magazines across the globe, felt like a waste of time to Bukowski, and he said as much to his longtime editor, John Martin. He also believed that making dozens of drawings for the special editions Martin envisioned for his Black Sparrow Press imprint drained his energy, unnecessarily so. Sometimes Bukowski exploded; feeling that Martin treated him like "an idiot," he would reply to his editor's demands with a sneering "yes, father." Interestingly, when both Anne Waldman and Allen Ginsberg invited Bukowski to teach at the Naropa Institute in the late 1970s, he turned them down. What mattered most to Bukowski was writing the next line, and submissions, paintings, and teaching gigs were but distractions. Writing was his crutch, he claimed over and over again.

At the very beginning of this volume, a young, unknown Bukowski asks Hallie Burnett for a job in *Story* magazine, and at the very end, barely a year before his passing away, when he was popular beyond belief for a small press author, Bukowski candidly thanks editor Joseph Parisi for finally publishing him in *Poetry* magazine after decades of steady rejection. These letters show that Bukowski was doggedly persevering, that no obstacle would hinder his hunger for success and recognition, that his writing disease couldn't and wouldn't be cured. As a very young artist, he methodically began to cultivate those literary traits that eventually turned him into the "Bukowski" persona that he happily perpetuated in his work. Reading these letters allows an insightful glimpse into his lifelong struggle to become a literary icon.

And now they are available to you, in all their raw glory.

Abel Debritto
Tenerife, Spain
August 2014

Acknowledgments

The editor and publisher would like to thank the owners of the letters here printed, which include the following institutions:

University of Arizona, Special Collections

Brown University, Providence, John Hay Library

The University of California, Bancroft Library

The University of California, Los Angeles, Special Collections

The University of California, Santa Barbara, Special Collections

California State University, Fullerton, Pollak Library

Centenary College, Shreveport, Louisiana, Samuel Peters Research Library

Columbia University, Rare Book and Manuscript Library

The Huntington Library, San Marino, California

Indiana University, Lilly Library

The State University of New York at Buffalo, Poetry/Rare Book Collection

Princeton University, New Jersey, Rare Books and Special Collections

The University of Southern California, Rare Books Collection

Southern Illinois University, Carbondale, Morris Library

Thanks also to the following magazines, where some of the letters were first printed: *Colorado North Review, Event, Intermission, New York Quarterly,* and *Smoke Signals.*

Last but not least, many thanks to Michael Andre, Gerard Belart, Anthony Linick, Christa Malone, and A. D. Winans for providing copies of some of the letters.